Blue Songs in an Open Key

Stories
Arya F. Jenkins

Fomite

Burlington, VT

ISBN-13: 978-1-944388-60-7

Library of Congress Control Number: 2018952734

Fomite
58 Peru Street
Burlington, VT 05401
www.fomitepress.com

Acknowledgements

Jazz, hard bop in particular, is an experiment, a leaning over the edge of time with sound. Thanks to the artists who ventured to do this with music and who inspired this collection. Thank you also Jerry Jazz Musician, an online zine in which these stories first appeared in their original form, and especially Joe Maita, for his constant appreciation and support of my work.

Contents

So What

Whenever I'm pissed off, I escape to the pit. Out the kitchen door, fists deep in the pockets of my tight ass jeans, I head towards the woods back of the house.

I cross the backyard, past Moreno, the poor chained up boxer. Rosa clinches his leash, pulling him close like a kid. Moreno tenses, cowers slightly as I go by, his spindly legs and stubby tail shivering at my wrath, ears perked, head cocked—*Was up girl, grounded again?*

Fuck you, you pig, I say, cause what is going on in my mind is getting bigger and bigger, and I cannot be interrupted by this canine nonsense. You dig?

I stare at the ground as leaves scatter to escape my ire. My shoulders hunch and I steel myself like a football player, letting nothing get in my way, snapping branches as I strut the path, a mesh of leaves and branches closing tighter, sealing everything out. I pop a cig butt into my mouth.

When I get to my place, I light up 'cause it's freedom there, it is home. Taking a deep drag, I crouch at the edge of a circle of dead leaves. One lone tree rises from the debris.

My mind goes over how they abuse me. I offer them my truth, and what do they do?

"Shut up, fool," my brother James, the football queen, always says to me. Always running up and down the stairs, his helmet on, trying to get in shape for games. The football queen.

"Flaca" or "Mexican Jumping Bean" is my mother's name for me. "A donde vas, flaca?"

"Nowhere. Mind your p's and q's ma," I say, just to mess with her.

"What does that mean? Why you so disrespectful to me, bean? What's wrong with you? You becoming, so, so American," she says, as if that is the worst thing. Since she found out her husband is not the man she thought she married, being an American is an offense. In marriage, you promise to be there. My father is never there. His appointments are with the world, not with us.

My mother and grandmama came to Washington Heights from Cartagena when my mother was 17. My *abuelo* had already been in the Heights for years – a musician, trying to make it. By the time his family arrived, he had fallen out of sync with them, or they with him. He and my grandmama spent years trying to sort things out, keep it together. Eventually, my grandpapi stopped playing his music and just drifted into mindlessness, and that is how he died, a *loco*. By then, my parents had married and moved to the Connecticut burbs, where I was born. I never met El capitan, which is what they used to call grandpapi. Cartagenans are wild, made crazy by the sea, my grandmama used to say, by way of explaining my grandfather's erratic ways.

My father grew up on a Midwestern farm in the wake of the Depression, an only child, driven to succeed. Work was like a god to him, and because of this, he pushes my brother too. One day I overheard him trying to bribe James to run for president of his class. Mind you, James was in the fourth grade. I don't think James took the bribe. I saw them sitting together in my father's study, James on the footstool at my father's feet, nodding a big *yes*, which to me looked like a big *no*. What did my father expect, asking him to do that, and did my brother only pretend to go along with his dreams and expectations? As far as I know, the only thing my brother ever chased is a football.

If we were talking, which we are not, I would say to my mother – So, you don't want me to chew gum, dye my hair, put on tight jeans, what do you want? But I already know.

"Respetame." "Calmate." She wants me to be like the "Little Flower," the saint, no joke.

To her, a gringa is no good. American girls smoke, drink, swear, and basically defy everything that is traditional and conventional—in other words, everything that she represents. That is not me. So, I am no good, a fracaso.

Not that I am my father's kid either. Do NOT think of me as *his* seed, that bullshit gringo who keeps trying to be like the BIG authority in the house. Ha.

Once, at dinner, I nearly caused World War III, saying Nixon is a pig, just to test my father, El Macho. He jumped from his seat, so pissed, his blue eyes bugged and his right hand did the one-two, up and back like he was going to hit me. His one-two made my mother spit a mouthful of rice and peas onto her blouse, she was so scared of him then. Of course, I just smiled at him. The fool.

"You better get right," says Frieda. My sister imitates our mother and would do anything to please her. She wears our mother's lipstick and puffs out her chest like she has something to show. Like who would look at her. She is just a kid, younger than me. She lets Rosa braid her hair. She is so caught up in doing what Rosa wants, she has like no personality. I feel sorry for her.

I imagine these accidents of fate, my so-called family, are like the little leaf I hold in my hand, a crusty little insignificant thing with tiny veins and nothing to show for itself. The thing I set fire to, watching its edges burn, holding it between my fingers until I can hold it no more.

I hold on until it burns. Then I stamp it out and go home. There are only two constants in my life, two things I must do. Home and school, and this is what defines my youth, being impregnated with bullshit.

At school, Sister P has us write a poem about the sea. I take my time, as this is not just about finding the right words, but an exercise in music. A few days later, Sister P tells us she tossed out our poems, as she believes we had our parents write them for us.

I try to remember what I wrote, my belly burning with resentment and rage:

The waves surge
Breaking into uneven lines
Of white dust
That disappear into infinity.

That is all I can recall, "surge" being my new word, found in the Thesaurus dictionary. So you can go to school, but you can't be a poet. That's what I learned from that lesson, Sister P.

Betrayal is everywhere, and I have to get this into my head. But every once in a while I am the fool too. Like choosing wallpaper. My mother took me shopping for it, and who knows why, possessed by some kind of nationalistic fervor, or maybe just a masochistic impulse, a desire to feel entrapped, I chose a psychedelic red, white and blue wallpaper design— fat, red flowers in-between blue vertical bars on a white background. Now I have this to stare at, and I swear to god, I feel like I am in jail.

Which, of course, I am. It's all I can do to keep from being driven nuts by my family. My mother takes my sister Frieda out to buy her a bathing suit and gets her a tacky tiger-skin design. Frieda is only 11 for chrissakes, and it looks stupid on her, so when Rosa has Frieda model the bathing suit for me, and asks me what I think, I tell her: "It looks stupid. Too old for her."

This was not the answer my mother expected to get, so she turns to me, black eyes beading, and says, "I hate you!"

Just like that.

I go to my room and sit on the bed, thinking of what she, my mother, has just said, hot tears welling, thinking: *Man, if your mother hates you, you are done. No mother is supposed to hate her child.*

But I know what I have done and why I am paying. I have abandoned my mother to become a gringa. To her that is the worst thing, unforgiveable, and she has let me know it.

So that is how it is, with everyone being under somebody's thumb in my house. Only once in a rare while do I feel like I have escaped. Like when I am with Tommy, my best friend who is like me. He is of age, has wiry hair and wears shades day and night. Skinny as a reed, his mama calls him. He brought Quaaludes back from Mexico, and gave me two to take with a gin and tonic he made for me. We hopped on his bike and went see *A Clockwork Orange*, me closing my eyes and holding onto his narrow hips like rain. Wind seared my face and we rode so fast, my bandana flew off my head, but I said, "No, don't stop. Keep going, keep going."

At the movies, I got up to get some popcorn and tried sliding my hand inside my pockets for some change, but couldn't, couldn't even find my pockets. That creep with crazy eye make up, the giant penises, the whipping in the rain. What does it all mean?

This world is full of incomprehensible images and things. On TV, I watch a soldier in what looks like blackface on a stretcher weep into another soldier's arm. Bullets ring through the air and there is fire everywhere in Vietnam and it gets to me. I can't bear to hear Marvin Gaye's song, "What's Goin' On," because it feels true. Because of this, because of all these incomprensibilities, I want to go far away, where there is no news, nothing depressing. I don't want to know about the war, or see suffering. I want only music and soul. Finally, when I find my father's special gift to me, a gift I take, I realize what I have always been walking around the house trying to find, like something lost. It is music.

This is where my father lives when he is home, downstairs, where, next to his desk sits a box of old records. On his desk, an ashtray full of cigarette stubs that obscures his college insignia is proof he was here, listening, his records taking him far away to a place and time he remembers. His music, I think, must bring him relief.

The album covers bear faces I don't recognize from another time. Thelonius Monk. Miles Davis. John Coltrane. Dexter Gordon. Why has my father never told me about them, or about this music? Was this what my father escaped into when he was my age? I read the liner notes and listen, and close my eyes, trying to imagine him through the years, feeling him out through the music.

Who was my father before he stopped listening to his music, then to my mother, then to me? Maybe, I tell myself, it was when all the *shoulds* came into his life. The shoulds of a wife, a job and children. I realize I too make up part of the wall of his bullshit. Time passes forward and backward as I listen.

For my 16th birthday, my mother gives me a peach blouse and a cake, with fewer candles than the year before. I swear she takes a candle off every year. She doesn't want me to grow up, only backward, until I become an infant again, needing her.

But my father's music, his secret gift to me, gives me a fresh understanding of how things are. Even if nothing changes and the reality of the world is the reality of home too. I stand in the hallway staring through the open door, as my father, wearing only his tennis shorts, straddles my mother on the bed, holding back her arms. Rosa screams, "I can't take it, I can't take it anymore!" My father shakes her by the shoulders, the holy medals on the silver chain around his neck dangling before her face.

"Get a hold of yourself, Rosa. Get a hold of yourself."

It's one long scream between them, a song I don't understand, a strange jazz cacophony.

But so what, I tell myself. So what. I am just a kid, not meant to understand everything, not even how it is between them.

Sitting in my father's study, staring at the ashtray of stumped out cigarettes, his worries, his loves and his pain, I sail on Coltrane, as if that's all there is, through *A Love Supreme*, investigating God with him. I read about the man, about bebop and swing.

But there are others too, and I get to know them. Nights, where there used to be poetry, there is now this. Now I escape on notes, the music in my father's study that takes me out to street continents, and makes me feel brave and hopeful again.

I realize what jazz does is make me think – not about separateness, but how things connect, interrelate. In my mind, fresh associations spring, all inspired by the music. In school, I listen to the music in my head. It jives with Sister P's clinking rosary and the sound of her clicker snapping the class into order. It jives with her hard-heeled step, and the cracking of pencils between her fisted hands when she's upset, and the sound of erasers smacking the chalkboard.

I hear jazz in everything, even the weather. There is a time in late winter, just before I split from home, when all

I can hear is Miles playing "So What" as I follow my own footsteps back and forth in the snow.

One day after school, I put on my Converse high tops and my father's trench coat and just take off, keep walking until I can't anymore. I hitch a ride to New York City and spend the night in a gas station bathroom, hunched in a corner, wondering what it would be like to be free.

I try to see my father as he used to be, as I have seen him since in snapshots, lean and blonde, before his hair thinned, when he looked a lot like Chet Baker, a pretty boy.

What do his silences mean?

I'm in Harlem, hanging by The Apollo Theater in the rain when my father finds me. B. B. King's name is on the marquis. I don't know him or the Blues, not yet. My father walks right up to me, and ushers me into a café and buys us both coffee. His eyes are red; his face, ashen. He doesn't take his eyes off me, and lights a Raleigh, his fingers trembling, and pours milk into my cup of coffee, which I don't drink. Who does he think I am?

"You okay kiddo? You're soaked with rain."

What does he mean? Who does he think I am?

"I'm leaving your mother," he says. "I'm sorry, kiddo. I'm sorry to have to tell you now, this way. I figure you'll find out soon enough. It's hard to explain why a man and woman separate."

I am shutting out his words, listening to "So What," the beat, in my head, the place where Miles' horn starts struttin'.

"Did you ever love her?"

"Of course I did. It's not about that. You have to understand. Things are complicated. I'm going away, I've got to sort things out."

"You always go away," I say, noticing a small fingernail-sized scar for the first time over his brow. Was it always there? Did he get it during the Korean War? When did that scar happen?

"Listen. Kiddo."

"That's not my name."

"After the war, when I came home, I wanted so many things. I remember one night, there was a bar called The Royal Roost, where all the great artists played. They would record for radio, but if you could go, you went. It was huge. A bunch of us went. Miles was playing, his back to the audience. It was something. It was real cool."

"You're just saying that. So then what?"

"That's where I met your mother. That's where we met. She came with her father. He was so cool, handsome like a movie star. He loved jazz, and I assumed Rosa did too, but she just came with him that one time. I don't know who or what I fell in love with that night, but Rosa didn't let go."

He looks at me like he knows me, head tilting. "I know you like jazz. You've been listening to my records."

"So."

He turns away momentarily then looks into my eyes. "It's because of you."

"Because of me, you stayed."

"Because of you I feel I should go."

"That doesn't make sense."

"You need a father."

"And what does she need," I say, thinking of her for once, my mother.

"She needs somebody too."

"I understand, dad," I lie to him.

"Do you?"

He takes my hands, searching my eyes, not seeing, his blue eyes watering. He's a different kind of man now than the one I have known, vulnerable, and a part of me wants to turn away, forget him. I don't want to see him like this. Not now or ever.

"It's okay, dad. I want to go, let's go home."

My father squeezes my hands, and he takes me home. A few days later, he goes away and never returns, and I imagine him going on alone, lost in his music. And in his absence, the silence and resistance he was become my own song.

Soliloquy

I am a bastard son of the late great Chogyam Trungpa, a Tibetan Buddhist teacher who came to this country in 1970, amassed many followers and bedded many women, among them, my dear mother. My parents never married. My mother left my father and moved with me to the Big Apple when I was still a toddler. My mother met and married a broker named Irv and had my sister Pearl, and my own father went on to become a famous teacher and big lush.

Among my father's actual accomplishments was starting a couple of Buddhist centers, but unfortunately what I inherited of his legacy was the drinking, and his Asian eyes and large ears. In Tibetan Buddhism, it's believed there are 112 physical signs of a Buddha or enlightened being, and, like my father, I am said to possess a few, such as elongated ear lobes and a mellifluous voice.

I'm fond of the word, mellifluous, which I learned from

my friend Abbie the year I got sober in Ithaca. We were both students at the Tibetan Buddhist center there. It was in fact Abbie who inspired me to stop drinking. I remember that night very well. I was in very bad shape, not having had a drink in a day or two. I was determined to stop, but was in a state of anxiety, the likes of which I had never before experienced, stumbling around the Commons, looking for someone, anyone to help me deal with my bad feelings. I stepped into a coffee shop, and there she was. I recognized Abbie right away from the Center. She was new in town, and, I thought from the first, very attractive—tall, lean, with pale blue eyes and dark, short hair. My first thought was she's a dyke, not that I asked.

"Hey," she said, immediately upon seeing me. "Myles, right?"

"Right, right. Listen, can I sit down? Are you busy? I could use a friend."

I was desperate you see, and right away we got to talking. I couldn't keep up with my thoughts. My shrink had put me on new meds that were screwing me up, so it was a really bad night. Abbie said, "Stick with me. We'll go to a meeting tomorrow." She was a recovering alcoholic herself, attending AA, and this was all I needed to hear. Really. I just felt the cushioning of a friend right then because the people I'd been hanging with in bars just didn't understand, and had no inclination to help me stop drinking either.

Abbie and I started hanging out, going to meetings, walking to and from Cornell and her place. She had a studio in a very cool duplex on Willow Avenue. We were both taking pictures, film then, in the 90s, and Abbie, who was in the Graduate Creative Writing program at Cornell, also had a photographic studio at the university which we both used.

It was a heavy year and a happy year for us both, the best and worst of times. Stopping drinking was hard for me, and Abbie was losing her mother, who was dying of some kind of cancer. We had this Buddhist existentialist thing going on, where we would hang together late nights in cafes, drinking espressos, talking about all the suicides, the Cornell law students leaping over the falls. It was like really bad. There were three or four that winter. The falls were beautiful and there was some poignant aesthetic in choosing to die like that, we felt.

Abbie said, "My brother died an alcoholic. That is also suicide." I thought about it and I had to agree that alcoholic drinking can be a kind of suicide.

I don't think that's how my father intended it, or how I intended it. Rinpoche, which is what he was called—it means revered teacher—drank in order to fit into this consumer society for which consumption is everything. I think he drank initially to relate to his students, or to have them relate to him. I drank to appease my nerves. Really. Once I realized I could get through a day without scotch, I was all right, you see. I asked Abbie why she drank and she told me it was to be close to her brother. She drank to feel close to him and to remember him.

"What made you stop?"

"I just realized one day it wouldn't bring him back. And, as you know, ultimately drinking makes everything worse."

I couldn't disagree with that.

Abbie helped me stay off alcohol, but unfortunately, I got her started smoking. I have been a habitual smoker since I was 13, and have for some years rolled my own because it's cheaper. When Abbie and I made the rounds of the all-night cafes, she liked to help me roll cigarettes. She would down two or three espressos to my five or six, and eventually we would both be smoking, sitting outdoors in the freezing cold, listening to songs by Natalie Merchant, who was newly solo, or Bjork, or Lady Day wafting out the windows of wherever we were into the pitch black night that we loved so.

I had a kind of a crush on Abbie. I would see her sometimes with this blond chick from the Center that I knew was gay, the two of them strolling hand in hand. It was kind of obvious, so there was nothing for me to do or say. But one night, when we were hanging out at Stella's, I said, "What do you see in me? I mean, do you find me attractive or what—do you know what I mean?"

"I could say it's all the things you are, but you remind me of my brother," she said. "You're a person of excess like Jake was. It was always everything or nothing with him too."

Her brother was an adventurer who left the country during the Gulf War, fled to Patagonia, where he started a new life and grew a family. I never got further from home than this, four hours from the city. I went to Paris in my 20s, like everybody who has artistic inclinations, enjoyed the architecture and history, took snapshots. I visited Tivoli once too with my sister, who had a boyfriend there. But the last thing I am is an adventurer. I am the kind of guy who will buy a hunk of cheese and a salami roll and eat these in a single sitting. That is adventure for me. Still, I let Abbie have her illusion.

Tuesday and Thursday afternoons we went together to an AA meeting, then we would hang together for six or seven hours at a stretch. We were both students of the universe, living mostly off stipends from our fathers. In addition to writing poems for her degree, Abbie worked in the local bookstore and was learning to play jazz piano. She was a jazz aficionado. I never heard her play, but she would talk about Monk, Bud Powell and others who had mastered the instrument.

"I don't know of any great jazz pianists that are women," I made the mistake of saying once. She looked at me like I had sprouted a third eye.

"Even if there was only Marian McPartland, that would be enough."

"Hmm," I would say. I was always trying to analyze her. She liked it when I murmured approval because of my deep voice. She would tell me, "Myles, your voice is so mellifluous. You should sing."

"I can't sing."

"But you chant."

"That's different."

"Okay. Do the Padmasambhava chant for me."

So I chanted for her. She really liked that. I think she sent a tape of me chanting once to her mother. The energy of the syllables is supposed to help healing. Abbie's mother was very interested in Buddhist philosophy, in everything I think that had to with Abbie, who was her only daughter.

Abbie would have stayed in Ithaca, I think, if not for the event of her mother's passing, which drew her back into the world, so to speak. What I mean to say is, she found a world here between the Buddhist Center and her poetry studies and Jazz U, which is what she called The Bookery. She discovered a lot of what she loved jazz-wise, listening to the assorted tapes friends brought there for her to play. There was always jazz music floating among the bookstacks.

One time, I stopped by to visit Abbie at the bookstore when we were both feeling kind of low. She was on break at the university and got the idea we should rent a limo and go see McCoy Tyner perform at Birdland in New York City. It was a preposterous idea, but she was very spontaneous, you see. I resisted at first, "Oh no. That's too much money." But Abbie was set on it.

"Look Myles, it's 400 a piece. We can swing it. McCoy Tyner is Coltrane on the piano, man. We have to go." It was winter, and I wanted to drink badly, had not received news from my step-father in some time and was feeling lonely. The prospect of hanging out for a while with Abbie struck me as pretty practical, and so we went.

We rented a limo that took us through the twilit mountains to the city. Our driver Aydin had started as a city driver and moved to Ithaca only a few years back to be with his Turkish wife's immigrant parents. They lived with them and had two children besides. Aydin said, "In my country, they call me Effendi. Here I am just Bud." He knew the city well, and waited for us uptown while we went into 2745 Broadway at the corner of 105th Street, where Birdland was then.

At the door, a humungous character named Lennie asked to see Abbie's ID, which at first she couldn't provide. "I should care more about driving and about this than I do," she said as she plucked her license from her boot, "but I don't." She had given her car away when she moved to Ithaca, so she rarely carried her license. I think it was more the way she looked that made Lennie detain her at the door. She had punked up her hair with this stuff called Three Flowers that might have made her seem like a freak to him. Abbie looked very much the beatnik to me in a black turtleneck and slacks, and, once we got inside, a lot of guys started ogling her.

The walls were covered with photos of jazz artists that I wanted to check out, but we were led to the bar, where we stayed. We ordered virgin cocktails, cranberry juice and ginger ale, and watched the place fill up. We hadn't been around so many people in a while, so I focused on everything and everybody. There was a woman seated overhead with long flaming hair like my mother had before she lost it to chemo, and like Pearl has, but I couldn't make out her face.

Pearl and I are very close. She has an apartment on the Upper West Side and studies art. When I visit the city, I stay with her and we pull all-nighters talking. She goes over lists of things to do while painting her nails black and says things like: "Do you think dad looks more like Pacino in *The Sea of Love* or *The Godfather*?" Snapshots of Irv as a young man cover one high wall.

"Definitely *The Sea of Love*," I say, then we both collapse, laughing.

Tyner was with his trio, Avery Sharpe on bass and Aaron

18

Scott on drums, and they performed some tunes from an album called *Soliloquy* on a narrow space set at the center of this triangle, which had great acoustics, although I felt like I was in a mausoleum. Tyner wore a neat mustache and classy white shirt, and his short, wavy, greased-down hair really shone under the lights. He was intense, smacking the keys in what seemed like an offhand way, the left hand sometimes leaping cat-like then coming down as if to chase the mouse of the right. From time to time, he would pull out a folded handkerchief to wipe perspiration from his brow. The bass player wore a maroon tie with a bass design on it that kept bouncing near the strings of his instrument as he played. These guys were very dapper and cool, the drummer with a ponytail and goatee, so graceful, he looked like he might be conducting.

Abbie fixed on Tyner the whole time, her hands sometimes playing along with him on the bar, her fingers like small, graceful soldiers. Once, she leaned over and said, "He's such a maximalist, like Coltrane. Did you know they played together?" A lot of tunes they played were by Coltrane.

In my memory, Birdland would be lit with blue lights and filled with smoke as it might have been when it was at Broadway and 52nd Street, the way Abbie had painted the jazz scene for me as it was in the bebop days, bluesy and vague, raw and familiar, even though it wasn't that way when we went. Even though I had grown up in the city, surrounded by jazz, I had never really listened to it or appreciated it until then.

Abbie and I were really close then, maybe because we had spent so many hours together, but also because I was seeing her in her element, lost in the experience of the music, closing her eyes, physically letting go in a way that was very intimate. During "Española," an exquisite piano solo, Abbie drifted with the tune and I went with her back in time to a place I missed without ever having been there. It was Abbie's love of the music drawing me in.

Abbie was pragmatic about religion—it was what you needed to get through life, but she was passionate about jazz. After that night, I began to think the essence of the soul like jazz itself couldn't be measured, was without boundaries, like the self and reality, couldn't be established either.

"What attracted you to Buddhism," I asked her once.

"I was raised Catholic. I like the colorful rituals. I don't know. I believe in life after death. It makes sense to me. And you?"

"I don't know. My mother used to practice. Maybe it's my way of staying close to her."

We put down a lot of non-alcoholic drinks and got drunk on the music, so when we stepped out afterwards, and found the streets wet after the rain, it felt right, like we were in Paris, characters out of a movie. Aydin was whistling away, waiting for us in the limo.

The whole ride home I tried not to doze as dawn crept over the mountains. Abbie said she imagined Patagonia looked like that, with ramparts of mist and purple sky. I kept blinking, trying to stay up. Then Aydin slammed the brakes to avoid a deer and we careened forward. It was really close. He missed the deer, but the trucker to the right got him and Abbie saw the whole thing. It really got to her.

I put my arm around her as she began sobbing, short, dry croaking sounds that cut right through me. "It's all right, all right," I said. "Everything dies. Maybe its next life will be better."

"I know, but it's so awful." Then she said the most child-like thing, "Why does everything have to die?" But what could I say to that?

I believe every relationship has that moment after which everything changes and this was it. I leaned close to her, so close I could feel her breath, which was sweet and made me long more than ever for everything I had not had and could not name. I suppose I meant to kiss her, although I had told myself not to try. She turned her head and I found myself staring out the window at the blur of the landscape speeding by.

"Oh Myles," said Abbie, pressing her forehead into my chest, "I just don't want to see it. I don't want to be there." It was as if what I had done or tried to do had never happened. She was closer to me physically then than she had ever been and furthest away too.

It wasn't until that night returning to Ithaca that I realized how alone I had been. I didn't have a girlfriend like Abbie did at the time. She was really the most important person in my life then, next to my sister, who I saw only rarely. It's funny, I didn't think to stop by Pearl's apartment, or spend the night there when we were in the city. It never occurred to me, or to introduce Abbie to her either. I didn't really want the two worlds, my past and present, reality and where I lived, to merge. I only wanted to return to Ithaca, which was pure then, covered in snow, an oasis of prayer and literature, poetry and jazz. Only once in a while did you hear of the tragic descent of human birds down the waterfalls, the failure of hope in what was really a never land. There were times in the winter when the snow was so deep, it was up to your knees as you climbed the hills to Cornell, and other times, walking through the Commons, just wind beside you, when you sensed in the echo of your footsteps some far away place calling, only to realize you were already there.

The Bluest Train

My friend Carl lived in a house full of ghosts with an evil sonofabitch brother who stole his shit, I mean all his shit. But Carl himself, man, Carl was good as gold. He would give you the shirt off his back—everything, and did.

I moved in with my ex-old lady across the street from him in the late 80s when I was drying out and desperate for a change. Marcy took me in, even after I had been such a dick. She knew it was the booze made me sleep around, and even though she had kicked my drunken ass out on the curb, she took me in once she saw I was sober and clean. By then, she was already shacked up with a polite, fat, slob who was everything I wasn't or would ever be.

Homestead Avenue, where we lived, was a pleasant street in a nice section of Fairfield called Black Rock, near the water. At the time, people were starting to navigate to the hood, although since then real estate prices have dropped due to the many storms—there have been too many storms in the area, man. But because of Black Rock's proximity to the sound, which is like the sea, artists and strange people gravitate there.

I noticed Carl right off the bat. You couldn't help but see him sitting on his porch with his supersized feet, head and limbs, a Franken monster. So I crossed the street one day to meet my neighbor, who looked a sorry sight—blackish long hair like he'd stuck his big muthafuckin' pointer in a socket. You smelled the brother, even before you finished crossing the street. I swear he wore the same red, plaid flannel shirt and grimy jeans night and day. I'm not a style maven, you know, but I bathe, man. I like to look neat for the ladies. My dark hair is receding but I comb it and, personally, a clean tee says it all for me. I am tan due to my Mediterranean heritage, but other than that man, I have often been compared to Chet Baker. I look like the man, although my teeth are still good. Once, a chick thought I was Black, and that was cool with me too. I like the fact that due to the way I look, I could belong anywhere.

So I say, "Hey dude, how you doin'. I'm your neighbor, Vance. Just thought I'd introduce myself." I stretch out my hand, and all I hear is, huh? Huh?

I realize the man is half blind behind those wire rim shades. He has one of those faces that hasn't seen a straight shave in ages. It's like a rat gnawed his chin and cheeks in places. Some scary shit. Still, I climb the steps of his porch and shake his hand, "Vance, man. I'm your neighbor. How you doin'? Anything I can do for you?"

"No," he says, his voice like music. It's low and so sweet. I've never heard a voice like that, that even in a word, no, can tell a whole story. I hear in that no: No, you can't do anything for me. No, I'm not doing so well. No, I haven't seen a stranger, much less a friend in ages. No, I'm not available for kicking, if that's what's on your mind. That kind of voice, man. Magical.

"I live across the street," I say, to place him in context.

"Oh," he says, extending his warm paw of a hand. "Carl. My name's Carl." Then, "Marcy lives there," and you could hear the protectiveness in that.

"I'm her ex, man. Vance. I'm living with her 'til I get my shit together. Can I sit with you a while, man? Wanna chew the fat? Mind if I sit with you?" Truth was, I felt I could have told Carl I was a muthafuckin' murderer and he would have said, "Oh," and let me hang with him. I was deriving immediate and great satisfaction from the fact, very clear to me off the bat, that whatever I was, whoever I was and whatever shit had happened to me, was no match for the shit that had happened to him, my new friend, Carl.

So, we got to jawing. I told him about my recent bout with alcoholism and that I was a musician and that seemed to get him a little excited.

"What kind of music," he says, boots shuffling.

"Jazz," I say.

"What instrument?"

"Alto sax," I say, voice cracking, me doubling over like I'm jonesing, for the fact was I had lost my instrument on a bender and was without music. But the man says, "Are you all right," with that mellifluous, chocolate voice. "Are you all right," in a voice that makes everything all right with its craggy kindness.

"Yeah, I'm okay," I tell him. "I'm just detoxing. You know how it is, your feelings go on a roller coaster." I was still sniffling and shit.

Then the man takes out a handkerchief, perfectly folded, but so fucking filthy that just to look at it would make a hobo cringe. I didn't know what else to say but, "No thanks, man. I'm okay." So we creaked back and forth for a little while on our rockers, getting adjusted to one another.

There were three rockers on the porch of the yellow house. Carl explained that in the afternoons, he usually sat with his elderly mother, who was recently deceased, and that on weekends, sometimes his brother, who lived in the house with him and worked as a supervisor at a nearby factory, would sit with him for a little while. Otherwise, he sat alone.

Carl told me he had collected and transcribed the notes of Charles Fort from The New York Public Library. The notes contained data about unexplained phenomena, blood rains, ghosts and shit, that couldn't be explained by science and that had been ignored or discarded by the establishment and scientific journals of the day, real gold, man. He told me he had done little else but work on this motherfucking transcription for the last 18 years. Every morning he rose at five, downed a can of kippers, walked down to the store for the paper, came back and sat with coffee before his Remington typewriter, his face glued to the cartridge, while he alternately fingered the notecards on which the original notes were, and typed what he saw. The pile of pages grew alongside him, and the days passed into years. Around eight o'clock in the evening, his mother would make him a meal of chicken or ham and rice or potatoes and canned beans and afterwards he would listen to the radio, then climb the steps to sleep, his six foot six frame curled and cramped in the boy's bed in which he had slept the last 40-odd years.

I sat back and closed my eyes, listening to him and to the creaking of rockers and to the breeze, smelling wafts of pine and something almost sweet floating from the distance through the trees. I thought, I could do this a while, sit like this in the middle of nothing. There was something about Carl that cut the bullshit out of any conversation. He was so truth-based, so himself, raw and broken, fucked up, alone and pure, all that. You didn't dare bullshit him or yourself when you were with him. It would have been blasphemy.

So then in the middle of a bluesy silence he says, like he's talking about a secret stash of pot or something, "Do you want to hear some music?" So I'm thinking he's talking about the radio, which I don't listen to much because you know most of it is shit, and I don't care much about news, man. Only news I care about is on the street, and I don't even care about that anymore. You dig? So I say, "No, Carl. I'd rather sit here and talk with you, brother."

Then I hear him get up with some difficulty, shuffling and shit back into his house, creaking the screen door open then letting it slam. All that was left in his wake was a stinky breeze and his wobbling rocker. I wondered how old the cat was. It seemed to me when I looked close, he wasn't so old, maybe 40 or so, my age. But when he walked, he was like an old man.

I kept my eyes shut until I heard the door open and close, he shutting it nicely then and walking like a regular guy back to his seat at which time he planted this album in my hands, John Coltrane, *Blue Train*.

"You shittin' right? You telling me, Carl, you own a muthafuckin' record player and albums like this and you're only just telling me now?"

He smiled then or almost did and said, "Yes." I wanted to scream and howl, have him say, yes, yes, yes, again and again. I wanted to pull out my hair and run up and down the street in my manic state. Really, it was like that, like god himself had come down and said, you have done a good thing Vance, crossing the street, and I am rewarding you.

So Carl and I became real buddies then. The man had Parkinson's disease, only recently then, and was nearly blind from cataracts. I spent the next few months in which I was doing all I could to stay sober myself, doing service with him because it was very clear to me at that point how Carl was indeed a train wreck. And believe it or not, that wasn't the worst of it. I had yet to find out the worst thing that had happened to my kind friend.

I drove him to Marcy's eye doctor, who performed the cataract operations so he could see, and to a barber, so he could get some human contact and get himself looking like a human being again. Once I had him sit in his ratty bathrobe at the Formica kitchen table while I did his laundry and dishes, which did not appear as if they had ever been done, the cups and plates crusted, and dusty, even. I figured, without a woman, Carl's mother, the house had deteriorated, not that it had not always been like that.

Carl told me the craziest shit about Fort's notes. Sometimes I couldn't help break out laughing. I didn't know how else to react. He told me the ghosts in Charles Fort's notes, which contained information about phenomena like falling frogs and disappearances and shit, were popping out of the pages and invading his house. But I laughed too soon. His house did have ghosts. Carl said he was sure his father was still hanging out too.

One day I was talking to Carl about music, how I got into it when I was a kid, punished for my big mouth, forced to stay after school to learn to read it, to learn discipline. Carl had just read me some of the notes, his face practically on top of the page, you know, because even without the cataracts, the man was just blind. I had heard some wild stories and so was telling him my truth, you know, my religion of rebellion. We were two men talking out their souls when suddenly this wad of paper comes flying at me out of nowhere. "Whoa," I say. "What the fuck was that?" Carl calmly says, "That's my father."

"No shit. Why would he do that?"

"He was an angry man who never wanted anybody in his house," said Carl.

Another time, I was stirring up Campbell soups, mushroom and clam chowder, into a pot in his kitchen and suddenly felt somebody shove me. Carl was in the next room. Nobody was there, man, not even his creepy brother, who was this small, skinny dude with a clump of keys hanging on his bony hip who had god delusions. We hated each other, man. One look was all it took to establish ourselves as enemies because he knew I liked his brother and would help him, and all he wanted to do was put Carl down. In the winter when he went out, he switched the heat off on his own brother, man.

Carl was the keeper to my entire spiritual world for almost a year. Every day, soon as I could, I would head across the street and make us both a cup of java, but what with those ghosts and shit, pretty soon I avoided going into the house at all. We mostly sat on the front porch. Carl would crank up the stereo and let the swirl of horns steer into the greenery and sky, while I read liner notes on the albums, smiling now and then to myself about what I was reading that I also knew.

Why those ghosts played helter skelter with my poor friend, I could not understand. Only later, did it make a little sense, and then I didn't think those ghosts were goblins at all, but actual motherfucking monsters from his past, men who had been blown to bits or gone to jail and in any case were rotting somewhere.

I had great respect for the unique way Carl had of looking at things and once in a while he would toss me a spin. One day he says, "Where would jazz be without the women?"

"You mean, Ella and Sarah?"

"No. Nellie and Alice and the Baroness." He paused, stroking his chin mysteriously. "And Zita."

"Who?"

"Zita Carno. A concert pianist who wrote about Coltrane, who knew what he was doing before anyone else did."

"So, maybe every great jazz musician has a woman inside him dying to come out." I thought that line was a gas and laughed, but Carl didn't. He just stared straight ahead and kept rocking.

In the days when he could see better and was younger, Carl had bought jazz records to keep himself happy and alive. He had all the tunes by Trane, Miles, Monk, Dizzy. We could have spent eternity with that music, in each other's company, but eventually things change as they do. I collected enough on my unemployment benefits to get myself an instrument, a beautiful, incredibly sweet and direct Martin Alto, as clean as I felt I'd gotten. Once I got that instrument I was off and running. The gigs came, and I left Marcy's, Homestead Avenue and my buddy. I was back in the game, only not drinking.

Five or six years passed. Gigs were going better than ever and life was sweet. Then I got a call from Marcy about her boy overdosing. Chip had been her only child from her first marriage and now he was gone. I came back to Homestead for the funeral. Marcy had saved my life, giving me a roof over my head, so I needed to be there for her, to return the favor. I also wanted to see how my buddy Carl was doing. He didn't use the phone and couldn't get to it fast enough when it did ring. In all the years I'd been gone, we hadn't exchanged more than a few words by phone. Once, through Marcy, I'd gotten a Christmas card with one of his cryptic messages—a quote by Fort, I presumed.

A couple of days after the funeral, Marcy took off with her couch potato Al to see his parents in Vermont and I crossed the street to hang with my buddy. The rockers sat empty on the porch, so I tried the doorbell, and when, after a few minutes, nobody came, I went indoors, the mustiness catching me short, bringing me back. I was carrying in all the freshness and verve of the world into this hole of sadness and neglect.

Carl was sitting in the kitchen, nodding off. "Carl, buddy, hey, it's me, your friend, Vance. What's up?" He was like an old tree nobody had pruned in my absence, and had started to droop and rot. He had a graying beard now and his hands were filthy. I had time, so without thinking too much about it, I just got to work, trimming his hair right then and there and giving him a good shave and a manicure and pedicure, as if that in itself would bring him back to life.

I did all that for him because I was sure nobody else would and I knew he was a human being, a great human being inside the train wreck of what you saw on the outside. Later that week I hosed him down in his backyard, giving him the first bath he had probably had in months and took him out for some joe, because it wasn't enough anymore to hang with him on that porch. He hadn't spoken to anybody but the man at the newspaper store since I'd last seen him. So, when finally he looked like a human being, I took him out in my '90 red Mustang GT, showing off what life had given me just for staying sober.

But it turned out to be a sad day, a really sad one. We caught the headlines in the store that Princess Diana had been killed in an accident, and Carl cried about it. I remember it was the same day he told me the other story too. I was getting ready to drop him off, and when I got to his place, I leaned over to open the door for him and he flinched. I said, "Carl man, I'm not going to do anything to you, I'm just helping you with the door, brother. Why are you flinching?"

"Because. Because of what happened to me," he said. So I sat back and lit up, ready for another story. Carl's stories were usually made up of no more than a few words, but the way he went from one to the other, slowly and directly with so much feeling, you were right there with him.

So the man tells me that when he was young, he was drafted into the army and even though he wore coke bottle glasses then and had only held a job for a minute at a gas station that had fired him, even though he was, even then, scared as shit of the world, he had to go. He got his uniform and went into training, this gangly, nerdy giant, and one rainy day, when the men in his barracks got drunk and bored, they found him and figured the best way to pass the time would be to rape him. I nearly swallowed my entire cigarette when he told me that. I tossed the butt out my window and sat up then.

"Man," I said after a while, after I had wiped away some of my own tears, the first I remembered in ages. "Man," I said, "And what did you do about that?"

"Nothing," he said.

"Does your brother know?"

"Nobody knows. Except you."

I reached over and patted him on his big shoulder then,

just patted and patted. I wanted to hug the man and bawl. That news just broke something in me. There was nothing more to say about it. I guess Carl had been high from all the attentions and joe and then brought down by Princess Di's death and this had caused him to share the awful truth he had borne alone all these years.

"That's why. That's why," he said.

"Why what," I said.

"Why I've always understood what it feels like to be a woman. Inside, I feel like a woman." I was to learn through my own research that indeed men who have been raped often feel vulnerable, and like women themselves, although not necessarily gay.

I didn't know what to do for the man and knew that in a short while I would be hitting the road again, so I went to sit on his porch again the next day. "Carl, tell me about your brother, man. What kind of a man steals his brother's things?" His brother had been jealous of his mother's preference for him. It was some crazy Oedipal thing. After their father died, the angry son of a bitch left his gold coin collection to his first born, Carl. But, when the mother passed, as Carl couldn't see and was helpless, his brother appropriated the gold collection.

"Do you know where it is?" I asked him.

"In the attic, where he keeps his Nazi memorabilia."

"His what? That's one screwed up motherfucker. Carl, listen," I said, because I knew then what I would do for him. "You tell me where that attic is and if those gold coins are there, I'm getting them for you, brother. You dig?"

"Okay."

So, sure enough, against my better instincts even, because I knew the place was haunted with all kinds of beings, I climbed the steps and went into the room across from Carl's that was his brother's. The shades were drawn, as they were throughout the house, and there were mysterious, unopened boxes and shit. I had to know what was in them. So I lifted the lid of one and saw old precious rocks. Then I lifted the lid of another and saw a small human skull. Then I stopped looking. I crept to the attic door at the end of the crazy motherfucker's room. I opened the creaking door, and Carl, who was standing in the doorway, said, "There should be a string to a light on the right," and there was, but no bulb. So I got my ass out of there and went into Carl's room, where there was a flashlight with dead batteries. We still had time before his brother got home from work, so I skipped down the street for some batteries and came back and got Carl's flashlight working and crept back into that dank box of cobwebs that was the attic. I found the coins in a small box within a brown box. Sure enough, 10 gold coins that were going to be worth something. We went to the nearest gold dealer and Carl got a few thousand for that. So the next day we went and bought him new trousers, shirts and shoes, making him look like a million bucks, so he even felt good enough to go with me to an AA meeting. After the meeting, some chick came up to him, all oohs and aahs and where do you live and all that, and I swear he gave her his phone number.

I left Carl looking like a million bucks, with me feeling

hopeful and practically buoyant with my good deeds for my buddy. A few months after that, I called and got his brother and heard Carl was now in a nursing home. I felt very depressed about that because Carl was still in his 40s, and everybody knows a nursing home is end of life. Soon as I could, I hopped over there, prepared for the worst, but wow man, what a surprise. It turns out the people in the place had done him good. He had not only needed care from day to day, which he was now getting, but many friends, and now he had them too. Man, he had a chick with a cane, a red-head, not bad looking either, with Parkinson's too, around his age. They were sleeping together! I couldn't believe it. Carl finally found a relationship in a nursing home! That man's life was some crazy shit. A few months after that, I visited him one other time before going on tour and because I was flying high not just from my life, but the fact that the train wreck of a friend I had known seemed to be coming into some good. But at the desk I got another surprise. I told the receptionist the room number, and spelled out Carl's name, and she repeated it then said, I'm afraid he is deceased. He had been hospitalized with pneumonia a few weeks before and never made it back.

I called his brother to confirm. It took a while to get hold of the motherfucker, but he said yes, Carl had died. He said the last words Carl had spoken to him were, "I want to go home." I wanted to say, clearly not to the home/jail that was living with you, motherfucker. Clearly not that. Maybe, home meaning to this bro, listening to music on the front porch. Maybe home, meaning Coltrane and Miles, Dizzy and Monk, swinging in the rain. Maybe, home meaning safety from the violence of this motherfucking world with its wicked lack of care. But I didn't say anything. I just hung up the phone.

Carl never said, "I want to go home," to me. Sometimes we'd be out, drinking joe, enjoying dessert at the diner, and he'd get stuck in his seat, due to the Parkinson's meds, which his doctors never could get right. We'd sit maybe 20 minutes or half an hour, him frozen as a stone, me joking to lighten up the situation. Eventually, I'd get him to stand, and he would be cramped, hunched, frozen like that, only gradually able to lift himself a little and walk. Eventually, he could speak too, and when he was back in the car, and I had the engine going, what he always said to me was, "Let's go somewhere. Let's go. Take me somewhere."

Whenever I think about drinking or about how far down a man can go, or how much he can suffer and still go on, or whenever I see some poor decrepit person on the street, it's Carl I think of. But in spite of all this, and all these memories I've shared, I never once thought Carl was poor of soul. He was the richest man I ever knew, with a heart of gold only a few of us are lucky enough to know.

I thought of those motherfuckers taking turns at molesting that poor sonofabitch child man, helpless and passive as they knew he'd be. I wanted to go back in time and cut their heads off with a righteous sword, every one. I wanted to take my friend by his lapels and shake him up. "You're a man, fight for your place. Fight for your place. If you don't fight for your place, you're nothing in this world."

It took me a long time to understand, Carl had no fight in him at all. He was in a class all his own. A gentle giant, but more. Although some part of him had let it go, the memory of that horrific attack had remained in his body, freezing him, separating him permanently from all.

For me, for a time at least, Carl had been a kind of home. We didn't talk about our sexploits and shit, like other men do. No man, we were beyond all that, into questions of the universe. We'd be sitting outside, taking in the day, and Carl would say, "What do you think?"

"About what, brother?"

"I mean, what do you think is possible?"

"Do you mean cosmologically? Or in a human sense, man?"

He would pause for a second. "Cosmologically, of course."

"I can tell you what's humanly possible, according to my own experience. But cosmology?—Man, that's your business."

"That's right," he would smile to himself, then rock back and forth, as if we'd come upon a precious key in our conversation, an illuminating point, beyond which it was impossible to go.

Epistrophy

Disenchanted leaves fell early through the trees the summer I left my life for an ashram. The path to the ashram snaked into the woods not far from Tanglewood and reminded me less of where I had been than where I was going with its rotund emphasis on kindness and formality—within a year I would be studying Buddhism in a monastery and teaching English at Cornell in Ithaca.

I was attempting to put a punto finale to the moneyed nonsense in which I'd lived too long in Fairfield County, and wanted to quell my fulminating instinct, my destructive fires and find some kind of peace and stability, even at the expense of boredom—which may have been expecting too much.

When I was a kid, I dreamed once of coming upon an empty box in the woods through which wind whistled. I'd wake up terrified, sure I was being consumed by wind or emptiness, this being what I understood since those days to be the human condition. No other dream save one other where I was being crucified and split apart while on a cross stirred so much fear and angst in me. Well, anyway, it was 1993, and I hoped to shake hands with some other understanding of emptiness, and perhaps even cultivate my spirituality while at Kripple-U.

The ashram was called Kripple-U by its residents, Kripple-U referring less to the style of yoga practiced there than to the crimping rules of the place, which included sexual abstinence. We were encouraged to hang with members of our own gender, which suited almost everyone, as almost everyone I knew there was gay. The women were girlishly beautiful and the men, beautiful and boyish, as if perhaps we were all stuck on some adolescent bridge. There was an understanding implicit in the air that many of us were balancing on some precarious inner edge.

There was for example the wealthy and beautiful Tessa, from Boston, with a successful business, children even.

"What are you doing here," I asked her one day as we decorated the main hall for a celebration. "Why are you here?"

"I'm afraid of killing myself," she said loosely, tossing a long, white ribbon into the air. I watched the ribbon spiral downward slowly.

"If you do kill yourself, that will be your main legacy, no matter what came before," I told her bluntly.

"Yes, I know," she said. "But I always think about it, which is why I'm here, trying this."

Another boy, adopted and anorectic, went on the longest fasts, stretching his limbs extraordinarily whenever he did yoga postures. I used to see him walking the long hill into town in flip flops, still in his whites, murmuring to himself, and that is how he haunted the place after he committed suicide, drifting among the trees, a specter of unfulfilled longing. He hung himself from a nearby tree.

I have never met so many lean, pretty, discontented people as I did that summer at Kripple-U, everyone there hungry for something and longing to appease that hunger. As for sex—as often happens, the thing prohibited became the sought-after prize. Sex happened often—in empty bedrooms, bathroom stalls, meditation rooms, even the sauna.

At the end of Jenna's 30-day fast drinking only grapefruit juice with cayenne pepper and syrup, we celebrated going out for sushi. Afterwards, at a gas station, I sensed a latent energy spiraling out of her as she assiduously cleaned my front windshield. She got me so distracted whispering in my ear as I drove back to the ashram, I swerved and hit a barrier, blowing out the left headlight and denting the front corner of my brand new GT. Back at Kripple-U, we raced the long, red-carpeted corridor into the first available room we could find, Jenna yanking me by one hand while massaging her throat with the other.

From time to time, just for kicks, I rented soft porn videos from a store in town and snuck them into Kripple-U. We lugged the lounge TV into our residents' room, where there was minimal space between two sets of bunk beds, and hunkered down over sesame oil-and soy sauce-sprinkled popcorn to watch naked French girls go at it on the screen, the irony being that all my girlfriends at the time at Kripple-U were French Canadian.

Kripple-U prescribed vigorous yoga, vegetarian meals and kirtan—a ritual where, dressed in our best whites, we chanted and swaying blissfully before the white-robed guru as he lectured us sweetly from his throne onstage.

The guru surrounded himself with an entourage of elders who had been with him for years. Many of them dressed in orange to commemorate their long status as celibates and often handed down fierce judgments on what they deemed our shortcomings. Suspicious of my independence and questions—"Why do you treat us like children?"—they put me to work alone in a windowless room transcribing teachings.

Six mornings a week I sat before a desk and computer, listening to the gentle, lisping words of the guru through a headset connected to a tape recorder. Once in a while, someone peered in with a smile or snack. Sometimes I took breaks to meditate, sitting cross-legged for hours at a stretch on a plush red carpet before a mirror. Some evenings after seva, I went to that room to draw or paint on posters. Once, Karen from California and I spent the night there, limbs entwined under a thin blanket, reveling in sensual comfort. In this way, I managed to turn that jail into a nest.

Weekends we swam in a nearby lake or trespassed properties to crash swimming pools, that being the one amenity unavailable at Kripple-U. Sometimes I escaped in my red mustang to Northampton alone. I liked roaming the funky cafes, bookstores and record shops, where I picked up Dexter Gordon's, Miles' and Monk's music. Nights, I danced in the gay clubs, crawling back to my bunk at Kripple-U in the wee hours, wreaking of smoke and decadence.

In October, most of my friends returned to their routines

in the world. I myself had no intention of going back to where I had come from, except to pull a few warm things out of storage and return fast as I could to the artist's studio I had found in Lenox.

Situated on the second floor of a white clapboard building on a side street in town, it had once belonged to one of Chet Baker's girlfriends, a singer. It had everything in it I wanted and needed: a small, narrow kitchen, rectangular wooden table and two chairs, and in the main room, a couple of lamps, futon and television set on a blue carpet. During the day, light fell through the windows creating staffs on which I imagined notes dancing when I listened to music. It was always jazz, Miles' and Monk's compositions, creating a counterpoint to my inner life.

Many nights, I sat, my back against the kitchen wall, pondering my future. I had not let go of a past that haunted me and was burdened by dark secrets I was loathe to share. What could anyone do about what had happened to me? No matter what I said or how I said it, the listener would look at me, not at the culprits, as the one with three heads, the one to be regarded suspiciously. How could I rein in my memory, turn the page?

Following a therapist's advice, I had sent missives to my parents while I was at Kripple-U, hoping against hope for some positive reply. None ever came. My letters may have been discarded, perhaps unread. Eventually, as if in reaction to a delayed guilt, my father sent me occasional checks encased in a blank note of denial.

I was born Frances Blakely, adding the III to be dramatic

during my Catholic high school prep days, when I aspired to little more than drinking myself to death. As a kid, I would imagine myself a lush and stumble around my room dousing myself with glasses of water—practicing, I suppose. Soon as I could, I started imbibing, anything to numb myself.

Drinking did what it does best, drew out my demons, and quickly got me expelled from school. Afterward, my parents sent me to a shrink, who, upon hearing of my antics—which included slicing my wrists when I was drunk—informed me I wouldn't "live to see 20." The next shrink, well versed in insobriety, dubbed me a character disorder. The one after that, bipolar. I made the round of rehabs until, as the AA saying goes, I became "sick and tired of being sick and tired" and stopped drinking altogether.

Sober, the dramas of the moment quickly dissipated and I endeavored to talk about the past—as I knew people did in therapy—but found I could not. I would open my mouth to deliver a memory and freeze, literally. It was not that I did not know what to say—a torrent of words awaited at the gate of my mouth, but I physically could not utter them. It was as if I was still under the spell of the willful child I had been who had sworn never to speak.

I had known people with more unspeakable pasts. My friend Devon's father used to shackle him and his younger brother to the kitchen radiator when they were kids so men coming to the house could sodomize them after paying at the door. Devon's younger brother overdosed on heroin and Devon himself joined a 12-step program. These are the sorts of people I have always attracted—freaks, drunks, addicts and deviants—because they know I will be both moved and unruffled by their bizarre pasts.

To this day I don't know of anyone besides myself who was sexually molested by her own mother as a kid, except for the writer Linda Sexton, whose mother, the famous poet Anne Sexton, was a twisted, talented lady, not unlike my own mother. What I remember most about Linda Sexton's book about life with her mother is the scene when, after Linda tells her psychiatrist what her mother did to her—she breaks down, curling into herself with grief, while her shrink does nothing.

What can anyone know about such betrayal without having lived it? My intention was to forgive and get beyond my mother's abuse and, what had been worse for me, my father's rejection of the truth and me. To move on, get through this dyskinetic dream called life. I wondered about these things, memory, dreams and my responsibilities to them as the days grew whiter and colder, and I lay out the tools of my survival—pens, paper and paints.

It was then in that studio, listening to Monk's music as I sketched and painted poems, which became a living breathing thing then because of the energy of the music and my will combined, that I began to sense a kind of humor in the universe, a kind of laughter growing out of the tragedy that it is to live. Monk, a crazy cat, dyskinetic too, made me laugh and I had no idea why. Here was someone who could barely put one foot in front of the other, but listen to his music, man, what genius. My only choice was creativity.

My whole life I had masked the reality of my mother's intrusions pretending nothing had happened. How else could I have greeted my tormenter, day in, day out, except by pretending nothing had happened between us those nights when I should have been sleeping like any child. During the day, we might have been strangers unless she deigned to parade my sisters and me in one of our best outfits to be admired in front of guests. Sometimes I acted out, prodding my sisters and friends in the chest and shoulder, as my mother would me at the start of our nightly game, but when I saw this elicited only anger in others, I knew enough to retreat.

I imagine it started as a way to practice rhythm, the Catholic method of birth control. Why else would she have left the bed next to her husband, entered my sisters' and my room in her sheer gown, lifted me out of my bed near the door, asked my sister sleeping on the upper bunk to come and take my bed while the youngest slept below.

On that top bunk, my mother and I were invisible to all. Only the ceiling watched. My mother turned her dark eyes on me then, malevolent and unrecognizable, not my mother's, as she began to prod here and there. I knew I could make no sound, show no fear, no giggles, nothing. Only remain where I was, allowing her to do what she wanted. I was afraid then, knowing instinctively what was to come that I could neither reverse nor stop. And then she did prod me there, in that place no one, not even my self, was ever to touch. Then she pulled me on top of her as she began masturbating. Pressed between her large breasts, I struggled to breathe. The intense heat, discomfort and strangeness of it all made me nauseous even though I knew I could not throw up or reveal my disgust. I did not want my mother to see it and therefore hate me, so I swallowed all I was feeling.

There was so much happening inside and outside at once, the energy too much, all of it, unspeakable. Then finally my mother let go an unholy cry, then throwing an arm across her forehead said, "I am sick, sick." And I said, "You are? Let me help." And she said, "No, go away." I turned so as not to disturb her, moving as close as I could to the cold white wall, it being the only relief then, the only kind thing, as it absorbed my shivering heat.

When I was a kid, I rarely slept and would lie in bed, arms crossed over my chest, always wondering if she might come, fearing she would, praying to that entity called God beyond the ceiling somewhere far away that did not hear me that I might survive, get through the night.

Some nights, desperate for rest, comfort or love, I got up and went to my parents' door, raised my fist to knock and froze, realizing, despite all I wished, that if I knocked she might be the one to answer. And I did not want her to be the one to come to me.

One night my father who was never there came and sat at the edge of my bed in his shorts, impatiently rubbing my chest too hard, and said "Sleep, count sheep."

"I can't," I said, then slowly, slowly, over the span of many minutes, all the while praying he would stay with me, I managed to get out three words. By then, I was no longer able to speak much at all. I had lost my ability to say anything, all things being a kind of lie and myself knowing lying was a sin.

"She…..touches…..me," I said, many years, many lifetimes in-between each word.

Grimacing, he turned suddenly in the direction of their room where she slept, indicating to me he had heard me, and my heart leapt, thinking he is there now, my savior, he will help me. Then, looking down at me, he said, "I don't ever, ever want to hear you speak of this to anyone ever again. Do you understand."

My eyes must have widened then with surprise, shock even, before I felt something leave my chest and then blood drain from me into space and myself falling. For many years, I did not feel anything and every word I spoke was a lie, the unspoken being the only truth.

It was drink that brought up those secrets I had contained so long, making the pain of holding on to what I knew so intense that something in me cracked again, the place in my mind refusing to let go, so that without the alcohol, slowly, slowly I began to spill into the world. Now an adult, with so much still unformed in me that had frozen, stopped, so early on, I could barely speak to my parents or have anything to do with them, they having forced me into such a stasis of denial, and how would I shape my own identity and survive their betrayal? And on and on this story went, with me struggling to rise above it. And music, the only balm.

To take breaks from that internal dialogue, I took walks through the wintry haven that was Lenox. Next door was an art gallery and I got to know its owners, and across the street, an inn, where I found work as a waiter. The two gay owners figured I was a guy, which was okay with me, as I was not only thin, but my hair still short from the ashram days. I served breakfasts and afternoon tea to rich white old fogeys and got decent tips, soon carving a routine to keep from feeling boxed in. One snowy night, I went to a New Age potluck and picked up a sweet blond guy to bring home to cuddle with against the cold.

It snowed so much that winter, the sidewalks became virtually impassable. You could barely make people out across the street, only colorful caps filing by behind a high wall of snow. Sundays, I skipped over to a local elementary school where this guy had a studio filled with wall-size oil paintings of giant whales and other sea creatures that he sold to corporations. He made a load of money from his art, but lived like a pauper, with a coffee pot and cot in one corner, and Sundays hosted an open house, painting nude models. He often slept with the models, so needless to say, his wife dumped him and his studio became his casa for good.

The artists who lived next door were from New York and spent their time between Lenox and Sarasota, Florida—she, with white blonde long hair and big, watery blue eyes; he, tall, with an orange-fake tan. He would look me up and down, not knowing what to make of me. Once I started catering and had to wear a tie, he started calling me Little Joe, that being his name too—perhaps figuring I was one of his bastard offspring. He collected stray cats too.

Anyway, Joanne of the soulful eyes and colorful outfits, liked my wily art that she dubbed Existentialist Picasso and hung some of it in her gallery.

"You mean expressionist, don't you, in which case I would be more like Jackson Pollock."

"No, you're more spacious than Pollock. Existentialist, boundless," she threw her arms wide, inventing new meaning for the term.

The apex of that long winter was Kurt Cobain's suicide in April, which shook everyone I knew out of winter's sleep. I was tired of my solitary reveries by then, so tired of counting family wrongs, they had become like sheep in my imagination. So, as snow began to melt, I started hanging with some young poets I met in a café. I had only just started painting, but had always written poems, and published some too.

The young poets were super bright, angry, politically-savvy, from broken families themselves and did not seem to question or care about my origins, proclivities or whatever. I fit in with them, and they with me, and we performed together in cafes and on the radio. A group of six whittled down to four that included—17-year old Zoe; the darkly handsome Garrett, then 19; and Jack, who was 20, addicted to Rimbaud and with whom I fell in love.

Jack was a strapping guy who wore holey jeans and tees, and had some beautiful fire in his blue eyes. Man, could he write, and how he inspired me to write that spring and summer. We worked on typewriters, enjoying the clickety-clack rhythm of the dance, conjuring poems in a school auditorium as we messed with mikes, echoes and our voices.

We discussed art and poetry, dadaism and surrealism and did a tape for blind students, throwing our entire bodies into improvisations in that auditorium like we were tossing die onto the wide-board floors of the universe. My poet friends were always pumped about something, "Torch, what do you make of this?" "What do you think about The Doors?" "What about Patti Smith?" I had changed my name to Torch while at the ashram, all to reinvent myself.

"Lou Reed and Patti Smith know tradition, but they expand boundaries with their poetry and music. They're jazz too."

"But they're rock 'n roll."

"Fuck the labels, man."

We got on this kick, examining everything we knew that went beyond itself, even religion, determining that Buddhism was the jazz of religions.

"Torch, let's read some Rimbaud," was always Jack's wish, Jack who fed on the highest words of the ages, mysticism, death and the mind's awakening from darkness, which is why he was the best poet among those kids, the most serious and most daring. I knew when I looked into his eyes or heard him read, his big hands holding up a paperback of poems, his longish hair dangling, that he would do anything for the art. He was a true artist.

Jack and I sometimes went to Northampton to see art movies, and afterwards walked arm-in-arm along the sidewalks not caring what people thought——whether I was older, and he, younger, whether we were related or not, of the same sex, or not, not caring of the appropriateness or inappropriateness of our bond, which is what it was, the two of us committed to art and poetry, and me, to jazz, which bridged the whole fucking world of inconceivabilities.

Jack, Garrett and Zoe took me to see the Grateful Dead and Phish. I took them to Manhattan on the train, knapsack straps across our damp tees and thin button down shirts outlining bony shoulder blades, fed bread crumbs to pigeons in a park and blew a few bucks at The Village Vanguard so we could experience jazz together. I said, "Guys, you have to hear jazz to know poetry." Tenor saxophonist Joe Lovano performed, playing Coltrane, Miles, Monk and Mingus too, along with his own originals in the dusky belly of the bar, while notes crisscrossed the air like secrets.

Only Jack dug jazz at first. Only he understood what I meant connecting jazz and poetry, the two stemming from great love and the ability to take risks with what you know to be true in the deepest part of you. So he and I started listening to jazz in my little studio, Monk, Dizzy, Miles, and Keith Jarrett, typing jazz into our poems. I wrote poems with a staccato fury—"I was born when jazz raged and a continent sang with blood, streets were caked with it," began one of my poems from that period that was published in The Café Review.

One time, when we were hanging in my studio, Garrett said, "we need a name." He said "syncopation," Jack said, "and anarchy," and we became that, using that name when we read Lorca's New York poems and Langston Hughes' poems in voices, swinging, fingers snapping too.

Through Garrett, I met a long-haired aesthete who had fallen for Garrett, although Garrett not with him, and who ran a store full of rare objects from all over the world in Pittsfield. Marlin understood jazz and poetry, Shakespeare and

Rimbaud, as he suffered over Garrett as over other pretty, unavailable young men. He wanted to put together a book of our poems on the high tech computer he kept on the third floor of his store, but Zoe and Garrett kept hedging.

"I feel like a book would trap us," said Zoe. "We need to experiment more."

"Maybe so," ventured Garrett, fingering his nonexistent beard.

Jack just kept writing into his notebook. It didn't matter to him what happened. Like me, he just kept writing.

One afternoon Zoe read us a poem she had written featuring strong female sexual imagery. When she was done, no one said anything.

"I don't care if you don't like it or think it's gross. I don't care."

"It's disturbing," said Garrett.

"You're a wuss," she said.

"Well it's not like I'm going to lose sleep over it," he replied.

"Then it's not good enough," Zoe said, storming out of the room.

Another time, Zoe said, "We need instruments." We went to Marlin's store and used his African drums and flutes, listening to the sounds drift up the high ceiling, transforming possibilities and words.

I ran the store for Marlin during the summer months as he scouted for precious goods in Africa, and he brought me back a black Moroccan cape—necessary for a poet, he said. Garrett and I alternated shifts. I'd watch him counting money, hair disheveled, the worry of ages upon his furrowed brow. I could see him then becoming a man for whom money would mean everything and the moment this registered, some tender need in me to give to him switched off.

That summer I alternated between the lilting songs of Loreena McKennitt and the high glass walls and brittle sun of a would-be museum in which wooden dolls from Africa, Moroccan capes and Tibetan vests, all seemed part of my heritage and ken, and the punk absences of jazz-inspired poetry—cruel and staccato words expelled out of hopelessness, helplessness and glee, hung on the fences of pages meant to represent a different, fresh aesthetic, although they were really the articulations of common human urgencies.

The hunger in Jack blossomed, and I let him go, urging him to grow beyond the pond of Pittsfield. He went to Syracuse, then Oxford on grants, disappearing in a wave of ether as we all did when fall came, as if we had all encountered the illusion simultaneously that we were made of greater substances separately.

A year or so after Lenox, Zoe dropped out of a community college, aborted Garrett's baby and ran away to Ithaca, where I was studying Buddhism. We hung out, talked, meditated and photographed the homeless kids in the Commons, one of which she herself became, tattooed and rabid to adopt her own renegade family.

I listened to Dexter Gordon's ballads on my headset, walking to and from my job at a bookstore in downtown Ithaca and while hiking up and down the hills to Cornell, where I taught English to visiting scholars. Dexter's tenor sax seemed to say, "Don't worry, don't fret, just listen to the love." Which is what his ballads were for me, a greater love, like Coltrane's and Monk's music too.

In Ithaca, contemplating absurdities and the universe according to Buddhism, the sacred sounds of mantras became my spiritual mother and father, transforming all that was capable of lifting me above my own suffering. Whenever I dwelled on the past, I continued to wonder what had caused this woman, my mother, to do what she had. I could come up with no answer. Only madness. And so to this, chaos and unknowing, I consigned her, to an eternal darkness that I would plumb with questions for the rest of my life. But the sacred could counter my obsession to know, infuse it with light so there might be some answers. I found true kinship in jazz and a way to transcend myself in sacred repetition. In jazz and Buddhism was the divine. Emptiness they both sang. All phenomena is emptiness.

One day Zoe and I went to the local movie theater to see *The Piano*. At the moment in the film when the jealous husband-to-be punishes his mute fiancé for her infidelity by cutting off her index finger so she can no longer play the piano, Zoe gripped my leg, whispering loudly, "I have to go. You don't understand, I have to go now."

I said "wait," as I was absorbed in the movie. Zoe insisted, so we stepped out into the alleyway, where she paced nervously, struggling for words, she with her head shaved, looking much like a nun or boy standing in the darkness that was brilliant after rain.

"What is it," I said, wondering what she was up to, myself on the verge of impatience.

"I couldn't watch. It was just too close, you know. I shouldn't have done what I did, shouldn't have."

"Done what," I said, not wanting to presume.

"A fetus is a thing, a child to respect too. Because we are all fetuses," she said, spreading her hands wide as she made her pronouncement.

I wasn't sure what she was expounding on—abortion, evolution, or both, or if it mattered. What I felt was her reaching beyond herself.

I remembered one time when we had been strolling in the Commons and I gave her my umbrella. Without missing a beat, she had passed it along to a homeless guy who used to walk around wearing a tattered raincoat carrying a briefcase stuffed with plastic bags. He was napping on a bench, oblivious to the rain, but Zoe opened the umbrella and secured it so it would protect his face. I had thought then she understood what I hadn't realized she did, that the world is larger than her, than all our individual pains. Since coming to Ithaca, she rarely talked about herself anymore, although she was still full of drama. I could see then she was growing beyond herself too.

That night in the alleyway, I waited for her to elaborate, she knowing she could count on my listening. But instead, she began dancing like a Greek, spreading her arms wide, sidestepping around me, moving to some inner tune. There was no music, yet I could see her lips moving, as if reciting something, and herself still dancing, tracing invisible shapes around me, larger and larger boxes.

Broad Street

The day I moved into Broad Street, the roiling waters of the Long Island Sound burst over sea walls along the Connecticut coast from New Haven to Greenwich, flooding Bridgeport so badly, a poor, emotionally disturbed man actually drowned in a sewer. At Seaside Park, water rushed across two parking lots, swirled around a few skimpy trees and headed straight for the historic set of row houses that included my basement apartment. It was early December as I arrived, two knapsacks in tow, only to find my new landlady Rosie and my neighbor Alice knee-deep in galoshes in muck, hauling out my furniture.

A week earlier, Alice had lured me with, "There's a vacancy next door and it's yours. Everybody's an artist here. You belong." I had felt the studio with its cozy rooms and sliding glass door leading to a private backyard would be a real step up from the third story modern monstrosity with no yard or neighbors to speak of I'd inhabited across town for a year. But here now was a true disaster.

Dressed in a navy pea coat, her grayish hair wrapped loosely in a red bandana, Rosie was swiping hard the surface of what looked like a Mazarin desk, as if bruising it might detract from the irreparable harm salt water had already done. She had the sturdy, slightly bowed legs of someone whose ancestors had probably picked potatoes and lived to be ancient, the sort of trait I wished on the spindly-legged furniture that already looked defunct.

I set my belongings on a high shelf against the far wall of the main room indoors and went to survey the damage. The stripped down kitchenette with its rustic cabinets and open, empty refrigerator had suffered minimally. But in the main bedroom, where a premature dusk had already settled, a once handsome Elmwood armoire now appeared to be sinking. Rising water smelling like a combination of rusty pipes and bad food filled the room, sending me outdoors quickly. There, I stretched my arms high, taking in the fetid air as if it was fresh and welcoming, then hunkered down to help my neighbors hoist my sopping mattress onto a big rock in the backyard.

We finished just as a starless, murky sky descended over all. As we embraced, Rosie invited me to Stella's. I had already heard of Stella and was looking forward to attending one of her soirées.

"When is it?"

Rosie snapped her fingers to indicate——"Soon as the electricity switches back on." Which turned out to be two days later. I almost missed living by candlelight.

Stella and her boyfriend Sven lived next door on the second floor of the last building on the block. While Stella worked all day as a graphic designer, Sven stayed home——re-arranging furniture or working out, I presumed. A strange, blond hunk, he had the habit of slipping through doorways by hugging them, as if he'd once lived in a space too small to accommodate him. He rarely stepped outdoors.

With its high ceilings, wall-to-wall bookcases, original artwork and colorful Buddhist hangings, Stella's place was an artist's dream, and when she held an open house, it was mecca. There would be a line of people clear to the door waiting for helpings of the fat turkey, stuffing, creamed onions, beans with almonds, squash, mashed potatoes, homemade gravy and cranberry sauce, cheesecakes, pumpkin pies, homemade cookies and brownies that Stella prepared and laid out alongside a steaming pot of hot cider with cinnamon sticks and bowl of spiked punch across a long table in the main room.

After the long enjoyment of eating, a few of us settled on hard-backed chairs in front of the fireplace in an adjoining room, and Rosie got down to grilling. No one had prepared me for it, and it made me deeply uncomfortable, although I pretended to be cool about it.

Where are you from? What do you think of the neighborhood? What do you write? Who do you read? When and where was Lena showing her photographs? Had she sold that nude of herself stretched across Saugatuck Brook? What stories was Robbie working on, had he written any new poems? Her questions were all about creative work, the most personal thing to me, and therefore felt most intrusive, although I relaxed a little when I saw that her routine applied to everybody, not just me.

Rosie reminded me of my father years ago. Whenever he was home from a business trip, and we sat together at the family dinner table, he would challenge us with current events questions, forbidding anyone to speak until the one spoken to had answered. It was like that with Rosie, nobody complaining, everybody doing as told.

In the 50s, Rosie had lived among artists and jazz musicians on Banks Street in New York's West Village, raising two kids on her own while her musician boyfriends played gigs and eventually took off to do their own thing. You could name just about anybody well-known from that period— Miles, Coltrane, Bill Evans—and Rosie would have a story about them, having not only seen these guys perform at the Vanguard and such places, but having partied with them too.

That night I was treated to Rosie's album of black and white images from that period that found its way into my hands. She had dozens of photos of well-dressed, sloe-eyed musicians perched on stools or rickety chairs alongside their instruments in dingy rooms or cafes. Many of them I did not recognize. But in one photo, a pale Rosie stood naked, save for high heels, a mask held over her eyes with one hand; a cocktail glass raised high in the other. Just to her left, Miles sat slumped on a chair, cigarette in hand, giving her a sideways glance.

"Miles was a bitch with the public, but a dandy with the ladies. They all loved him," she said, telling us nothing new.

"What a grand time the 50s must have been," I said.

"The end of a decade is when all the great artists die, having spent their greatness on us. Pres left us in '58 and Lady Day in '59," she observed.

"But Joplin and Hendrix died in '70," somebody else chimed in.

"Which kind of marked the end of time," said Lena, and a few people nodded to that.

"No more music after that," said Rosie.

"Rock 'n roll, man, the Beatles, the Stones," said Robbie.

"Joni," said Alice, wryly.

"Maybe so, but more and more instruments playing at you not for you. Nothing subtle, no attempt to work things out like jazz. Just lashing at the world, boring, loud shit, not for me," said Rosie.

"Real artists die with the public," said Stella.

"And media," said Robbie, himself a journalist, the only one besides Stella that I knew had a fulltime job.

I had seen Robbie before, at a café reading I'd been to with my friend Ruby, who is also a poet. After she and I had each read a short poem, Robbie went up to the mike with a manuscript thick as his arm and proceeded to lay on us the entire first draft of a novel. "Mailer complex?" Ruby whispered to me, and I laughed. At Stella's, Rosie changed the subject.

"Did you hear what that idiot, Dan York said at our last block meeting?"

"No, what?"

"He said we should just leave our drug problem to the po-lice."

"Really?"

"He did."

"I thought we'd already done something—taken up a collection?" Stella asked demurely sipping a glass of wine.

"Oh, we're on it. You can bet on that," Rosie stabbed the pillow on her lap with a knitting needle—she liked to knit while chatting. "Would somebody get me another glass of wine before I have a conniption just thinking about that whole damn business."

"What business is that?" I boldly inquired.

"Some nasty drug-dealing mother-fucker sold bad drugs to a neighbor's kid, who OD'd and died. Right across the goddamned street. In our neighborhood."

"That's the truth," said Robbie reaching around me for the joint Alice was passing.

"That's too bad," I said. "I guess drugs are everywhere," the irony escaping everyone.

"Maybe so, but that shit sure ain't comin here," said Rosie, loud enough for people in the next state to hear.

"You got that right," echoed Alice.

"So what are you going to do?" I asked.

"Oh, we'll do something, you can bet on that. Cause we know nobody else will. Right kids?" Rosie looked around herself for confirmation.

"You sure about that dealer, Rosie?" said Robbie, extending a burning pipe to me. I waved it away.

I was still riveted on Rosie's photo album when I felt Billy's bristly cheek brush my own. Stella brought out more food, and there was another repast, after which some people took off with leftovers. After that, those remaining got too stoned to talk and I was able to do what I love best, which is just listen to music.

It was Bill Evans that night, *The Solo Sessions, Vol. 2*, recorded in New York City in '63, but newly released. I was thrilled by the experimental nature of the album, as he was improvising in tenths and obviously challenging himself, striving for poetic brilliance on his instrument while struggling with his addiction. I read the liner notes, listening to Evans in a way I had not listened to anything in some time, so that I felt the world open up for moments beyond the mundane sounds of running water in the kitchen—pots, pans and dishes being jostled, washed and put away by our hosts, beyond the walls even. I left Robbie, Sven, Lena and Alice stretched out on the Indian carpet, gazing stony-eyed at the ceiling as if at a great design there.

Another time at Stella's, my friend Nabi brought over his double bass to accompany me as I recited a few poems, and Billy joined in, drumming quietly on a stack of books and flipped-over pan. I was so glad Billy was there, his very presence reminding me to stay sober and clean, as he and I were the only ones in that group that did not indulge. We kept our sights on one another and caught a buzz anyway, as that night the pot smoke was so dense, you could barely see in front of you.

I was drawn to Billy, whose quiet confidence reminded me of my brother. Originally from Georgia, he had not been in Bridgeport long. Stopping here, newly sober, to take in a view of the sound and smell the sea on his way to a job further north, he found he could go no further.

Billy's swagger turned me on, that, and the fact he never let anybody, even Rosie, put his back up against a wall. He would answer Rosie's probing questions with his charming, southern, "Yes ma'am's," and "No ma'am's," with a simplicity and aplomb that cut through just about anything. His replies felt personal, but they never gave away a thing.

Underneath a well-worn army jacket, Billy wore a green gold scarf, the color of his eyes, and under that, a scruffy tee that gave away what he did for a living. If you ever saw him on the job, you would more than likely catch him stop what he was doing under a car hood, run his gorgeous hands across his broad chest wiping them free of grease so he could shake hands with somebody who'd come by asking for a favor. Whenever he came over to see me, I'd slide the glass door open to the backyard, letting our cigarette smoke blow out into the frigid night while we read our poems aloud to one another. Some nights he showed up in his truck and just honked—two quick honks then a third—because he didn't have a phone, or want one either.

I'd hop into his motorized ashcan, which is what he drove, and we roamed the neighborhood, listening to the humming darkness, the noise of slamming garbage can lids and chattering insomniac neighbors on stoops, and shift-shaper dogs and cats along the sidewalks slowly taking color and shape as we circled the hood. Billy had a penchant for driving cars without any headlights on at night, before that signified something evil in the hood, before gangsters started doing it just to get some stranger to blink his lights, so they could follow him and kill him. Now and then, we caught the glimmer of a blade of steel or a handgun whipped out in the heat of an argument, which sent a chill through me.

Sometimes we rode all the way to New Haven and café hopped, reading and writing poems together. Billy read from *Leaves of Grass* and the works of Robert Lowell, his deep, gravelly voice comforting me, while I read Neruda's and Langston Hughes' poems. I loved being with him, although our short history was like a roller coaster.

The summer before I'd moved to Broad Street, he called one night drunk out of his skull begging me to meet him on a beach. I wouldn't of course and asked him flat out why he'd bother calling me knowing I would turn him down if he was inebriated. He said something to me then that hit me like a two by four——"I called you because I'm a man with needs. Not one of your hermaphrodites, but a real man with real needs."

No one had ever said anything like that to me before, and it pulled me up short. After a brief marriage and divorce, I had become close to several men with whom I was intimate although not sexual. Afterward, I had to ask myself whether I was de-sexing them in the process of befriending them on my own terms. But at the time, because there was a ring of truth in what Billy said to me, I hung up on him.

After Billy got sober, we did wind up fooling around on Fairfield Beach. It was a beautiful spring day not long after my brother had died of the same disease that could have claimed Billy, and I was feeling low, wanting to be close to someone warm and tender. As we lay on the sand, Billy kissed me and I rested my head on his shoulder while caressing his hard cock through his khakis. He said something then that stayed with me too. "With most women, the closer I get, the further I want to get from them. With you, it's the opposite." He kissed me then, his warm mouth lingering, teasing, tender at first, then plumbing me for all I was worth. He was a great kisser, tender and simple, the way it never actually was with us, unfortunately.

When Billy drank, he got into terrible fights and wound up in jail and I wouldn't have anything to do with him. I don't flatter myself that he quit drinking on account of me, but I happen to know he stopped the day after making his drunken plea over the phone that I rejected, asking me to join him on the beach so he could read me his poetry. Did I mention that was part of the lure?

Billy was at the center of everything then, pulling me forward into the future. We would wind up in New Haven together for a time, until his longing for the south, and mine to move on, got the better of us. As it turned out, all the people on Broad Street I thought would play a key role in my life stayed peripheral—Robbie, and Lena, who also came to Stella's and had lived in my apartment before me until a rich uncle died, leaving her a trust fund that allowed her to get an apartment in New York's West Village, which is what she had always wanted. After that, whenever she came around, everyone wanted to get close to her, as if her good luck might rub off on them. She sat wrapped in a white shawl Rosie had made for her at one end of the love seat at Stella's, looking beautiful and languid, her long limbs entwined around herself, enduring the steady rain of flattery that came to her from everyone vying for her attention.

And of course there was Alice, who always struck me as kind of invisible. Thin, mousy-haired and grave, she exuded little confidence or appeal, but was always there to help, so you couldn't ignore her. She had dark, prodding eyes that fixed you with either an adoring or despising glare, nothing in-between. Truth was, she scared me a little.

We had met a few years back, in the days when I had a decent job as an adjunct teaching creative writing at a local college, and Alice was waiting tables, and studying Reiki and bodywork at night. We met while working part time at a feminist vegetarian restaurant—Alice, washing dishes, while I put together salads. Alice had just moved to Broad Street then.

She was an artist too. Her neat, watercolor seascapes hung in an uneven line along the dark hallway of her basement apartment, which was under Stella's and next to mine, although I never saw art materials of any kind there, so I figured art with her was a thing of the past.

The Sunday after my first neighborhood soiree, Alice had me over for tea, and I came over, feeling a little hung over from the exposure to all the smoke and weed at Stella's the night before. I thought tea might be just the thing. I was no longer into getting high with drugs, that being old news for me. I could no longer tolerate it. I had been clean and sober a few years then.

Alice was a freak about Joni Mitchell and, while not into jazz herself, knew I was. First, she played Mitchell's collaborative effort with Mingus, which I had not heard. I half listened, drifting with the tunes, but not totally into them, while Alice went on about Mitchell, listing her albums in the order in which she had heard and liked them, this being her way of discussing music. At some point, she lit a joint and offered it, and I just shook my head and refused.

After the Mitchell and Mingus album, she switched to Keith Jarrett, *The Koln Concert*, and we talked, or rather, I did about improvisational work and Coltrane while Alice seemed to disappear into her couch, either bored or stoned or both, I couldn't tell.

At this time of my life, the early 90s, I was enamored of all things experimental, so it was jazz I hit on and stuck with when it came to music. I was exploring Ornette's *The Shape of Things to Come*, which I listened to over and over again on a cassette player. Ornette had become a private minstrel reorganizing and sparking the dormant places inside, connecting my body and mind. Whenever Alice saw me sitting with a cup of espresso at my kitchen table, she would slide open her back door, so Mingus's *Ah Hum* or Ornette's music could drift over to me from her stereo. That was the love she extended, for which I was always grateful.

I wrote, exploring my own darkness with my pen, encountering as I plumbed it, weary characters full of angst and rage desperate to escape reality. I lit their cigarettes, heard their footsteps following one another across damp cobblestones at night, listened to their dramas and registered their complaints. Hyped on caffeine, I disappeared with them into alleyways, back streets and dens of iniquity, where they challenged one another and death.

As I reveled in the film noir of my imagination, old demons came back to haunt me. I itched to get high again, to allay the fear and angst that were, I then felt, being triggered by energy seeping in through the walls of my apartment from the nervous systems of others in the neighborhood with whom I was now connected and who were conspiring to put an end to my sobriety—if not in actuality, at least psychically. I was convinced of this.

I had friends in recovery who disapproved of my being in the hood. "You're playing Russian Roulette with your sobriety," Steve would say. I had known him since the days when I was married. He and I had worked for the same company, gotten sober together and hung in together through his many relationships and my divorce. He was a protector, but I was bothered that any time we got together, he would harp endlessly on what he perceived as my "bad move." He wrote long lists of positive thoughts for me to recite to myself in front of a mirror, lists that I kept tucked under my pillow. On rare occasions, I let him or Nabi take me to meetings, but the truth was, while I lived on Broad Street, I didn't much pay attention to AA or my sober buddies, although they turned out to be right. Broad Street was not safe. I had learned that early on. But those were the days when I felt sure art, literature and music could trump anything.

I had been on Broad Street only a few days when, one afternoon I became distracted by the sound of fireworks—a party happening? I set aside my writing tools, grabbed my jacket and stepped outdoors to check out what was going on. I had taken no more than a few steps along the sidewalk when I heard a window creak up and Rosie's voice calling, "Hey, where you going?"

"A walk. I think there's a party somewhere. I just heard fireworks."

"That's not a party. It's gunshots. Get back in your apartment. You can't take a walk in this neighborhood."

Rosie's words set me straight for the moment, but didn't totally register. The whole incident just felt like a momentary deterrent, nothing more. I had come to the garret with the aim of nourishing my imagination. Even if the energy on Broad Street always felt thick and dark as pipe resin, the darkness was conducive to creativity, wasn't it? I had a support system of sorts here among my neighbors, a view to the stars through glass sliding doors, a private backyard, and all the inspiration I wanted and needed in music, conversation and my own ideas—these were the thoughts that won out.

A few weeks after that, determined to do my part as a new neighbor, I hosted a party, inviting everyone I knew to it, something I have not done since and hope never to attempt again.

I invited tough-talking ex-druggie and alkie friends from AA; rock and roll and jazz musician friends—some active, others recovering in 12-step programs. I invited poets; exes, who were from the good side of the tracks in New Canaan, Stamford and Darien; even an African-American model I had just met who looked like a princess. After an AA meeting, a few of us had gone to a café, and she had tossed this line to me across the table, "I have never slept with a woman, but if I do, I want you to be my first."

I figured I'd stick to tradition and get a modest-sized turkey for the party. I had no intention of competing with Stella, but couldn't get away from the idea that what everyone expected was a turkey. Unpretentiously, I set bowls of chips, raw veggies and dip around the room for hors d'oeuvres, and served sliced turkey, stuffing and beans on paper plates for our repast.

My neighbors rolled joints and drew somewhat self-consciously from pints and fifths of bourbon and vodka discretely tucked inside paper bags so as not to tempt those in recovery sipping soda from their Styrofoam cups. As my modest space filled, the potheads gravitated outdoors, encircling a Mother Mary statue inside a rock enclave in the backyard. Indoors, a trio of jocks from my pool party days in New Canaan got rowdy, hollering stories at one another, saluting the air with beer bottles, while a gaggle of writers and former students sat in a huddle on the floor beside them, attempting to read poems aloud to one another. In the midst of this, Eve sashayed her lithe self in a wide brimmed hat, thin arms chock full of jangling bracelets, back and forth like a pendulum. Out of the corner of one eye, I thought I saw Alice, head in her arms, crouched under a table, but I couldn't be sure.

In the middle of "The Circle Song," which Rosie put on and my friends in the hood were grooving on, my friend Paul, who had brought his guitar, pulled up a chair and began his own performance of an original——I could tell it was that by the way he enunciated every word. His song drew most of the women over to his corner. The more that females closed in around Paul, the louder the jocks got, and the wilder and more desperate the poetic discourse. Now the diversity of sound was at its peak. It was close to 11, and Mingus's "Boogie Stop Shuffle" was playing in the background, following the party's crazy tempo when a small thing happened to change the course of the evening. Either ignoring or unaware that Stella and Sven were an item, Paul put the make on Stella.

Sven began hollering incoherently in broken English while lunging at Paul, but, although taller and better built, he was clearly not a fighter. Paul held him back with a stiff-ened arm, while hoisting his guitar out of harm's way. The jocks cheered, a crowd got ready to mosh. Then, just as someone yelled, "Take it outside," I heard sirens and two cops were at my door. Dutifully, I switched off the music and promised to send everyone packing.

Alice and Eve helped me clean up, sweeping up cigarette butts and putting furniture back in its place. Afterward, Alice came up to me, her eyes wide and out of focus, as if expecting something. I gave her a loose hug, thanked her and sent her home.

All night the tenderness of Eve, her sweet flesh and warmth, competed with incumbent realities. As often happens with me when I have sex, all I do is think of what I have to do, and this night my frustrations raced like caged mice on a wheel—the longing for a decent job, a way to write without worries. I wanted to get high again too, and was now searching my mind for that right drug every addict dreams of that would saddle me with neither hangover nor consequences. I was aware of "getting one step closer to drugs with my stinking thinking," as those in AA would say. Until then, I had kept those desires at bay, knowing if I let them surface, I would have to confront the reality of my situation on Broad Street. But that night, the palliative of Eve allowed them to rear their ominous heads.

In the morning, Eve still in my arms, I gazed out the rectangular window overhead, where I normally contemplated the promenade of legs and shoes on their way to work and saw instead a repo man under my Honda, attaching it to a hitch.

"Look at that," I said as if we were watching something on TV. Eve huddled closer.

"Don't worry, babe," she said. "Make you a deal—I'll take care of your vehicle, if you drive me back to Stamford and spend the weekend with me." Eager to take a vacation from reality, I let Eve take the wheel, so to speak, and off we went to la-la land. It wasn't until the second or third day playing house, when I felt I might go loony from the constant rotating of an overhead disco ball and blaring hip hop in her bedroom, that I decided it was time to get it together.

Eve was less than a month sober, and messing with someone so early into recovery was considered a big faux pas in AA. I made up my mind to do the right thing, and at the end of the weekend found myself kissing away her crocodile tears while delivering to her the program cliché that I had to "let her go to grow." An old boyfriend of hers had called while we were together, so I was sure no hearts were broken. She was probably on the phone with him or someone else by the time I got to my car.

Back on Broad Street, I sat for a moment in my vehicle, pondering how quickly good times dissipate, then how best to keep my car safe parked where it was. Stella had told me she always left her car windows down, doors unlocked, so nobody would be tempted to steal anything. In the midst of contemplating this, a lunatic came at my car out of nowhere, hair flying, slapping a note so hard on the windshield, I thought for sure it would crack. My jaw dropped as I watched her hop into her car, slam the door, and take off before registering who it was—Alice, an Alice I had not seen before.

Her note read: "You are a two-timing son of a bitch bastard. I want my tapes back." It was in this way I came to realize I had to pay a price for having had a girlfriend that was not her. Too late, I saw where Alice had been all along where I was concerned, and told myself I should have known better, should have seen it coming. But how was I to have known? I had never felt sexual toward prim, vague, asexual Alice. Had I known she had a crush on me, I doubt I would have behaved differently, although I might have paid her more attention.

At Stella's the following weekend, Alice played the hurt stone, staying far away from me as she could. I pretended not to care, but it was hard not to notice the glacial shift in the room. The universe was sending me a message and it was not in code. By hurting Alice, I had upturned my own place in the hood. Rosie did not so much as glance at me, attending to her knitting with extra detail, and I realized quickly it was she, Alice's ally, moving the ice, making the decision now to detach me from the group.

But the group was undergoing a general catharsis, I was soon to learn, as something else had transpired, far more sinister and important that concerned everybody.

"So, what's up with sneaky Pete?" someone asked.

"Oh, he's gone. Won't be coming around no more. We got rid of that sonofabitch real good, didn't we," said Rosie, stamping her cigarette out into a yellow ashtray.

"Mob style. Back of the head. Boom!" someone elaborated.

"Where d'ja bury him?"

"No burial, no way. We had our friend take him to the dump. We set fire to him."

Robbie stood, putting both hands up in a resisting gesture. "Whoa," he said, "I don't want to hear this."

"You were there when we voted," said Rosie.

"I didn't vote," he left the room lighting a cigarette.

"We have the best neighborhood watch in Bridgeport," said Rosie, still looking at the yarn on her lap. Everybody nodded, agreeing, looking down, examining fingernails, avoiding eye contact with anyone, so the gravity of the exchange sank into me. It was the one time Billy was not there to act as buffer, so there was no protection from the seeing and hearing, from my registering completely what had gone down. I left soon after, like someone leaving a burning building, not caring whether I had said goodbye to anyone.

It was the same night Bill Evans played a song for me, as I sat at my kitchen table, trying to make sense of what I had just heard. The smoke of ages, illness and death permeated my living room, congealing into shapes, with Bill Evans at its center going over all of it with me, his way.

It was him all right, beautiful though gaunt from drug abuse, a limp cigarette protruding from the right corner of his mouth. A new moon reflected on his glasses as he played "On Green Dolphin Street," just for me. I recognized it immediately, although I had missed the first eight-bar section. He was keeping harmony to the treble of LaFaro's bass, although I could not see him, or Motian on drums either, his perfect trio. While Evans' left hand was agile on the keys—he was a leftie anyway—I could see the fingers of his right hand, two or three of them paralyzed from shooting heroin, only occasionally striking the keys. Still, hunched over the piano with his usual intensity, his playing seemed completely natural. I closed my eyes to just listen. Evans' sound was beautiful and pure, and this, the true rendition of the song. As I wondered whether he was playing on Glenn Gould's Steinway, I saw him nod affirmatively in my direction.

I began to dwell on another performance, that of my peers, which was not unlike a jazz improvisation, a marriage of minds, but its effect had been narcotic, leading me to deeper somnolence, poisoning me. As a group, my artist friends had agreed to take a life, collectively ridding the neighborhood of what they had determined was vermin, hiring somebody to do it. I had been so deep in my distractions, I had not perceived what was happening, or picked up on their casual righteousness about it. I was no longer in a world of art and possibilities, but one of danger, intrusion and death. Now Evans, in this place I had adopted, supplicated me only to listen, a pure artist's plea, and I would do that, keep honoring the music that way, for it was clear I had not listened before, not really.

"Can you play Broad Street," I asked, and he indicated he could not. "There is no Broad Street," I heard. Then he went back to grunting over the keys, like Monk, Jarrett, and Glenn Gould, at the end, shifting the key up a third, midway through the out chorus, making the piano sing as the song disappeared slowly and him with it, his presence joining the trees and elements beyond.

Then there was nothing left but the simple items I had brought with me, books on shelves and other knick knacks, tools with which to dream I would take with me to another destination, continuing my artist's life elsewhere.

Heat

1. Savoy Blues

Mercies would have put blues on the menu if it could, but that was a province of the kitchen, where I worked four and a half months too many. I heard actual blues music and caught a gust of air conditioning early in my shift whenever I snuck through the dining area to use the guest bathroom before customers arrived, passing the line of booths next to the orange and black walls on which hung colorful modern paintings of jazz musicians and the shiny oval bar at the restaurant's center that was as cool, slick and neat as the kitchen was hot, mean and funky. As I hung over the toilet, pissing the hot, bitter pee of someone who drinks too much coffee and has too much stress, I let the music of Muddy Waters, John Lee Hooker and Louis Armstrong seep into me like a balm. Sometimes my sneakers did a one, two, before I hoisted up my jeans reminding myself: that's your enjoyment for the day, sister. Get ready, it's time for hell.

Once the ticker tape with orders started rolling in then flying, you forgot about everything but popping wings or whatever into the fryers and getting orders out quick without burning yourself too bad, and plating everything nice and neat. Once we got cookin', you didn't think about your kidneys or anything else, you just stayed focused. If you forgot to tuck a Styrofoam cup full of something iced at a corner of your station to stay hydrated, you were shit out of luck. Even with a cold drink nearby, you rarely had time for a sip. Even when it wasn't crazy busy, the manager was always on your ass to do something—as if we didn't have enough to do already, as if putting up with all we did and making $8.50 an hour while doing it was stealing from the establishment.

The prep gals at Mercies put together soups, chili, mac and cheese, deviled eggs, potato salads; assembled tomato beds and prepped fried green tomatoes down in the basement. They did the stocking too, hoisting huge sacks of flour, rice and sugar onto high shelves and lugging 50-pound cans of oil and hefty pots full of greens or soup upstairs to the dark, narrow kitchen. After working their butts off all day, they went home to kids and husbands or boyfriends, and did the same shit all over again, only in smaller measure.

I've been cooking professionally 20 years, starting out prepping at a restaurant in Georgia after Arliss left me when Sally was two. As far as kitchens go, things haven't changed a bit in that time. Women are still bitches and scrubs where men are concerned.

2. March of the Hoodlums

The hoods I worked with at Mercies got treated like royalty. They slouched in late, droopy-eyed, nasty-tempered, more hung over than you would imagine it was possible for a human to be, itching to argue, looking half the time like they'd slept or passed out in some seedy alley in their black uniform jackets and stained checked pants.

I expected management to get on their asses for their being late or looking like shit, or for their attitudes, but no such thing. The manager Abel couldn't wait to pat them on the back and call them a rock star in the kitchen.

I was the only female upstairs working the fryers next to scrawny, toothless young druggies and overweight ex cons, every one of which was off the wall. Second night on the job, two of them got into a fistfight, due to one owing the other money. The older one quit and got hired back the next night after the one who had stayed, whose girlfriend had just had a kid, got fired. Day after that, the one hired back was sent to the emergency room with heart issues, forced off his feet for a month and therefore off the job—at 31. Classic kitchen drama.

Bottom line is you don't take a restaurant job in Warren, Ohio, because you want to join Top Chef, but because you're desperate. Restaurants attract people who can't get hired anywhere else, ex cons whose records don't matter in a kitchen, or women who think they were made to have kids, take orders and cook. Some of us, however, don't take shit, even if it looks like we might. We stay quiet, don't talk unless spoken to, and aim just to get by under the radar. We do the job, usually better than most, long as you stay out of our grille!

Stress is constant. You have to put orders out fast without a fuss, fix problems in seconds, act like everything is cool all the time. But working in heat and under duress turns people into all kinds of monsters. It made the guys I knew horny as hell.

3. Chasin' the Gypsy

Some grabbed their crotches when they saw you, or smacked your booty when you passed by. One or two got in my grille and asked whether I was "giving my gravy." If they had balls, they asked you out, and of course then you had to find an excuse. "No, I've got a hot date with King Kong after work, no can do," I told Lenny once. Long as you had two legs and arms, and your own teeth, you were up for grabs at Mercies.

I was the only woman working in the kitchen there, and the only woman with my own teeth. All the others, younger than me, wore false sets, or none at all as their sets didn't fit. Some days, the ladies in the basement looked like a bunch of grannies. Fact was, some already were, at 41 and 42. It wasn't only poverty that had got to them, they had more kids than me, had been married longer, and so were naturally worn out.

Jackson claims I winked at him first time I laid eyes on him, the afternoon I was led into the kitchen and introduced to the crew. He might be right about that. I was in the mode after all, wearing a tight blue dress, my hair down for the job interview. I remember Jackson poking his big black head under the shelf where the orders are placed, welcoming me with his sly mug, and after pushing his glasses up at the bridge with his thumb, turning that same thumb up to his buddies, a signal I was in. Abel spent most of his time hiring, as staff quit all the time, although you pretty much had to set fire to the place to get your own ass kicked out.

I was very deliberate wearing that blue dress, letting my hair down and putting in contac lenses to make sure I looked as attractive as possible. I needed the job as I had just walked out on a gig a little further down Route 422. In this industry, you not only live paycheck to paycheck, you try not to talk about where you've been. It's just bullshit to managers anyway, as they only care about how you perform for them. Anyway, I let my hair down to get the job, but once I got it, pulled my hair back into a ponytail, put on my glasses and my hard veneer. Jackson always looked at me like I still had that blue dress on, like he knew what was underneath. He made me smile and blush at once. I couldn't help liking him.

When I first met Jackson, he still had a black box around his ankle, was still under house arrest, and lugged it around like a ball and chain. You saw guys with black boxes around their ankles all the time working in kitchens. But Jackson was polite, which I immediately respected. On account of this, I listened to him and went to him whenever I had questions. Sometimes, if orders started flying in, he would help out, tossing shit for me into the fryers, putting his hand on the small of my back as he went around me, respectfully helping me get plates out at my station. This sort of thing I found very attractive. He had other nice habits too. Like whenever I ran outdoors to check my cell phone before Chef came in, or whenever I clocked out, Jackson would always follow, lighting a cigarette while hanging over the banister just outside the back door, watching me get into my car, as if looking out for me.

4. Wild Cat Blues

Once in a rare while, when the weather turned bad and it rained like monsoon season in India, it got slow at Mercies, and I took over the watch indoors waiting for orders to come in while the guys formed a huddle out back next to the dumpster and shared a joint. Dope of any kind was not my thing, and I had no inclination whatsoever to visit prison, especially after the stories I'd heard. Not that Chef Randy gave a damn about a little smoke, he himself being into bigger things.

Most of the time, I worked next to Lenny, tattooed with snakes, scorpions, eagles and skulls from his neck to his ankles. He was artistic, having designed some of the eagles and skulls himself, and liked showing off his designs, some of which were in intimate places, and each of which had a story. Across his fingers in ornate lettering was tattooed, Son of Satan.

Lenny had been in prison too, after being caught driving from Chicago to Pittsburgh with 50 pounds of pot in his car. When his windshield wipers stopped working in the rain, he pulled off the highway. A cop spotted him, and that was it. Lenny said, "If you smoke and are a young male driving a shitty car, cops will check your vehicle." He got seven years, but only did three, getting out on good behavior, he told me. Lenny was 33 going on 70. I never questioned his lack of sanity, just nodded at whatever he said. He had a crazy streak in him a mile wide that you would have had to be blind not to see.

It was Lenny gave me the recipe for how to make hooch out of orange juice, like they do in prison, and how to tattoo yourself with a staple inside a pen and burned Vaseline that turns into soot that you scrape off a piece of cardboard after you burn it. I said to Lenny, "All that self tattooing must have been painful."

"When you're alone all the time, you got nothing better to do."

Man, I thought to myself, you could have read a book.

My first weekend shift on the fryers, they put Lenny to work with me, and right away he got to talking big, or what he thought was big, bragging how he liked to spend every minute of his time off shooting "whatever I can find" in the woods with his gun.

I'm a meat eater and don't deny it, but don't talk to me about shooting critters that have done nothing to you then act like you're a big man for doing it. That's just bullshit. I crossed out Lenny with a big X in my head when he started talking like that. Not only did he gab ceaselessly about killing things, he'd whip out his buck knife from a sheaf at his hip, and show us how it cut through meat, "like butter." His hands were big and so familiar handling that thing, it sent a chill through me. Whenever he snacked on anything, he used that knife as utensil. I didn't like it one bit.

That first night working with Lenny, I would not even look at him so it was not hard to read my feelings. He got back at me taking over when we had an order so he did all the frying and plating, but when it got to be real hell in the kitchen with a dozen or so orders coming in at once, he just disappeared on break for a good 20 minutes, which could have been disaster for the whole kitchen. Next day, when I complained about him, Abel just told me to let it slide. Turns out, Lenny was one of the biggest rock stars.

Besides Jackson, the only other dude I could tolerate at Mercies was the dishwasher, a gentle giant named Lester, whom we called Samson, Sammy for short. Sammy's ex-wife was a big drunk with a long list of DUIs, so Sammy was raising their twin girls, Samantha and Julie, who were five. He was a real doll. Sammy would cart big boxes of goods from trucks to the cooler, take out garbage, and sweep up too, in addition to what has to be the hardest job on earth—washing restaurant dishes. He had the saddest eyes, but always kept a smile on, even while working like a dog, his tee soaked through with sweat. I had a soft spot for him and would fry him a side of wings or bacon, slipping them into a bag for him whenever Abel wasn't around.

Sammy's niceness and Jackson's attentions balanced out the sheer terror I felt sometimes working next to Lenny, who was a time bomb just waiting to go off. You can't trust somebody with dead eyes, which Lenny had. I was so intent on seeing the good side of everybody, I almost forgot about those eyes.

In order to get along, I finally made a point of looking at Lenny, noticing his downturned mouth, his feet that turned in, and the sadness he wore like the weight of the world on the lonely hunch of his shoulders. Then I started being a little nice to him, patting him on the shoulder, shooting him a compliment now and then over the way he handled burgers and ribs. His strong hands pressed down so hard on the steel spatulas to make meat cook fast that his burgers actually spurted blood. One day, Lenny confided to me he liked cougars, me thinking like an idiot he was referring to tigers, not realizing until later while lying in bed with a book that night that he had been referring to me, an older woman, a cougar. So then I knew it was time to temper my compassion, even though it brought some relief to see I was now on his good side.

5. Keep Your Temper

Chef Randy joined us about a month after I'd started at Mercies. He was a real dick, but as he was taking over after a long vacuum, he was given a lot of leeway with us. His first day on the job, he ripped into a young kid who was using too much pepper on the sides of beef he was massaging downstairs—"hey dipshit"—so the kid and his mother, one of the prep ladies, told him where to go by not showing up the next day or ever again. What idiot introduces himself to staff that way.

Truth was, Chef Randy was a drunk and addict who would spend the first 20 minutes of every day in the bathroom getting high. You never heard a toilet flush when he was "occupied." One day I went in after him and saw a white spray of dust on the sink that was definitely not soap so there was no mystery about what he was doing. Most of us had "been there" or been in relationships with people who used, so we knew what we were up against with him. Not that we could have done anything. We were up against the wall, constantly vigilant whenever he was around. He was so full of himself, walking in late, always sucking on a can of Coke, always propping it somewhere that it would spill, always blaming somebody for his messes. He acted like his real job was to criticize everybody, but when he got pissed or authoritative, all you noticed was his Faux Hawk hairstyle bobbing like a Baby Huey, making him look ridiculous, laughable even. Still, we all knew better than to cross him.

I stayed out of Chef Randy's way, but was always torn between trying to be nice to the guys I worked with that I found hard to like and turning my hard side up to them because these guys didn't know what to do with nice except fuck it and that wasn't going to happen. Finding a balance wasn't easy. There was nothing simple about my relationship with them, or their relationships with each other either.

Jackson always acted like a friend, but didn't miss a beat where Lenny and me were concerned once Lenny and I turned the page on our initial dislike of one another. At first, it was kind of cute, sensing that extra current of possessiveness and jealousy the two got going over me. The minute I'd start paying attention to Lenny, he'd be all over me, trying to help me out his way, repeating with his slow drawl, "Y'all have to do it like this," showing me how to do shit like I was a newbie. He would really get into that when the kitchen was slow, abandoning his station and sticking to me like glue, and it occurred to me that was probably his way of courting.

One day Jackson got bored watching this and started acting like a porpoise jumping up and down behind Lenny to catch my eye. He cracked me up, so I started tossing him fries that he caught in his mouth. He actually caught them. I could feel the heat of Lenny's ire next to me percolating, but I didn't care. I wasn't married to either of them. Besides, if I was going to work my ass off in a thankless job, I was going to enjoy myself whenever I could. After the game was over, Jackson sidled up to me and said, "You know in the blues, food means sex, like offering your cabbage and shit."

"Yeah and you prefer French fries," chimed in Hector, a Latin waiter with slicked back black hair and a favorite orange shirt he liked to wear who was expert at overhearing everything. "Ha ha ha, ha ha ha," Hector began banging the back of his round tray like a drum. "Anybody want to try my cabbage? No, I'll take your French fries. Ha ha ha."

"Fuck you, Hector. You nothing but a mambo queen," Jackson told him. Hector did a samba, heading out of the kitchen, still beating the drum.

Those two, Jackson and Lenny kept different kinds of eyes on me. One day, I took off the rubber band around my ponytail to adjust it and saw Lenny crane his neck, taking in the sweep of my hair, which I could see brightened him a little. Jackson on the other hand was vigilant, a protector, even though I always felt that was the way he hoped to get to me. Even an ordinary man can turn into a genius when he makes up his mind to win over a woman. And sometimes, even a smart woman who knows the score can act like a fool.

6. Back Door Man

Like so much in life, everything boiled down to what happened one night, one event that determined all our futures. It was early fall between the lunch and dinner shifts and we had the back door open, letting in breeze while Jackson and I danced to Muddy Waters' "I Got My Mojo Working," which the bartender Alec had turned up for us. Jackson was going around kicking up his heels while pretending to play a guitar behind the counter. I laughed as he skidded onto his ass on some grease, cracking himself up, got up and kept up his performance. Then Lenny showed up, looking pale, wearing his mean snake eyes. I watched Lenny strut over to the register to clock in, then head downstairs to grab his coat. In a minute he was back, coming around behind the counter with a fistful of bags of burger buns that he thrust into a shelf under his counter and frozen burgers that he stacked inside a cooler drawer under the stoves. He nodded at me. I nodded back, took a sip of my iced tea and went back to watching Jackson, who was singing: "Got my mojo working, but it just won't work on you/I wanna love you so bad till I don't know what to do," while Lenny stared straight ahead ignoring all like he was just waiting for something really important.

"You think you are some hot shit, man. I bet you thought

that in the joint too," said Lenny.

"Got my mojo working

"But it – uh uh – just won't work on you."

"Aw, let him be, Lenny. We're just having a good time."

At which point, Abel came around hollering orders, "Is that pork ready. I need to have somebody pull the pork. Lucille, is your station ready to go for tonight, we have a couple of big parties coming."

"I'll pull pork, boss. I'm all set up," said Lenny.

"Hey, man," Abel came around to Jackson and put his arm around him, "Go wash the sweat off your face, buddy," and again, "We have two parties of 10 at six tonight."

I went downstairs, taking my time getting a couple of extra sacks of sweet potato fries from the freezers before coming back up. I could hear the ticker tape starting as I climbed the stairs.

"Pork fries," Lenny called out, so I popped some into the fryers figuring we were getting started early that night. The clock over my head read five fifteen.

I hauled out the fries, seasoned them, poured them into a basket, went to get four ounces of pulled pork and was sprinkling that on as Chef walked in, his face red from drink and possibly wrath as he watched me garnish the pulled pork sauce with bits of greens and bacon.

"What are you doing with pulled pork fries. I ordered a sandwich."

"That was you, Chef?" said Jackson, who ran the sandwich station. "Why didn't you say so."

"I said so. It's on the ticker tape. Pulled pork sandwich.

Hello!!" He looked at me. "Can't you read."

"I called it out," said Lenny quietly.

"Pulled pork sandwich," Chef yells at me again, even though the sandwich department is where Jackson is standing on the other side of Lenny, even though Lenny called out "pulled pork fries."

I shrug.

"What are you, hard of hearing? Dumb?" He yells at me again, and I feel myself blushing.

There was no mystery to Chef's outburst. I knew what it was about. After grease from the fryers had wrecked my glasses, searing the anti-glare layer so it looked like I was seeing through snow, I had asked the accountant in the office downstairs whether she might talk to Chef about having management help pay for a new pair of glasses, or even goggles to protect what was left of my glasses that had cost me close to $400-dollars and many months saving up to get years ago. She must have talked to Chef right away because that same day, the day before the one I am telling you about, he came right up to me, spraying his vodka breath on my cheek at the peak of the lunch hour while I was juggling several orders. "Grease from the fryers didn't do that to your glasses. That grease don't have no preservatives. There's no way grease did that to your glasses and no way we are paying for it."

Until that moment, everything that had happened at Mercies——from fights between workers to squabbles over orders——had happened at arms' length, not really to me. My glasses getting ruined was a disaster that was in my face, literally. And Chef getting in my grille about it was just plain wrong, so I let him know it.

"First of all," I said, "Of course this grease has preservatives. Secondly, that has nothing to do with the fact that hot grease splattered my glasses and ruined them. Thirdly, since you don't believe this hot grease ruined my glasses, I will have the optometrist at the eye store call and explain to you exactly how it happened. Tell you what, I don't want to talk about this right now. Bad timing. Why don't you just get your face out of my face and stick to what you know." With that, I kind of waved him away with my left hand.

Until that point, I had not spoken more than two words at a time to Chef—good morning or good night, and yes chef, or no chef. Until then, Chef Randy might have had the idea I was a meek woman doing my job the way he wanted me to do it, and would never have to worry about me. After my small tirade, he went away quietly, but I knew when I saw him the next day, the day that everything happened, that he had murder on his mind where I was concerned and would be out for my blood. So that's what his yelling at me was really about. Payback.

"Hey, you deaf or what," he yelled at me again.

I was that kind of crimson that grows steadily and threatens to combust if nothing hinders it, while trying to stall my mind, which was telling me to just go, go. But I had done that already somewhere not long ago, and I wasn't ready to leave Mercies.

"Hey Chef, I just said I told her 'pork fries'," said Lenny.

"I don't give a shit. Shut up, meathead."

"What the fuck," said Lenny under his breath. I could hear him huffing and puffing. "Nobody calls me that," he shook his sad head.

"She's the one who did the order." Chef pointed at me like I was running from the scene of a crime. A part of me was starting to laugh a little inside seeing I had an ally, somebody I hardly expected to be there for me under such circumstances. It sort of tickled me.

"No need to talk that way. No need," said Lenny.

"Hey, meathead. If I want your opinion, I'll ask for it," Chef said again.

At which point, Lenny reaches for Chef's coat with his left hand, pulls him forward on top of the shelf where we planted orders, reaches back with his right hand, and simply, like it's something he's done plenty, plunges his buck knife between Chef's eyes, turns it once to the right and yanks it out. Then he wipes the blade on his jacket, slips it off, and just heads out, re-depositing the weapon in its sheath at his side. Chef jerks back, hands wild and quivering, eyes bugged like an animal watching its own slaughter, blood spurting everywhere, and drops jiggling in his own juices on the grimy floor just as Lenny disappears out the back door. Then Jackson runs around the counter calling out, "911, call 911," although, of course, it's too late for that. The waiters and bartender are now hovering over Chef Randy, hands stifling their mouths, while I stay frozen trying to remember what it was happened, what it was that was said, my mind a speeding train, going I don't know where.

7. Baby Please Don't Go

"God in heaven," I heard myself say, just as the sirens started.

I would tell you that men in blue took statements from Jackson and me before sequestering us, so investigators could grill us, riveting into our minds what had transpired that night. I would tell you if that's what happened. But it didn't go that way.

It was Jackson pulled me out of my stupor and led me outdoors. We passed men in white and men in blue rushing in. I looked back one last time and saw Abel looking around like someone crazed, like someone had just dropped him from a starship, and he was falling fast in space.

"Jesus, Jesus, what happened?" I said, and Jackson kept repeating, "It's all right. It will be okay." We stood there in the darkness that felt cold to me then, Jackson with his arm around me.

A little while later, I think I said, "He will never let them catch him alive. Never."

"I know that," Jackson said. Then, "It's nice out, but you can't see no stars. Come on now, I'll buy you a drink. I could use one and I know you could too."

I took my apron off then, depositing it in the trash bin next to Jackson's like there was nothing else to do, like it was the last thing we would ever have to do, and followed him to his old Lincoln.

A Man's Hands En Clave

For a long time Hector hid his broken heartedness about having nothing to say behind an attitude of "I-don't-give-a-shitism." From the time he was a teen, his favorite expression was "I don't give a shit," and he doled this line out often along with his lousy attitude to virtually everybody but his parents.

His parents were hardworking Cubans who had escaped to the U.S. on the Mariel boatlift in 1980, when Hector was only four. If Hector knew anything, it was that the one thing his parents deserved was his respect and his love, which he did his best to give them in his way.

He showed his respect by not speaking to his parents in his typical fashion and, whenever he was with them, demonstrating his love by accepting his mother's food and his father's taste in television, without a word.

Where his mother's food was concerned, this was hardly a chore for she was an exceptional cook, always serving up the Cuban dishes he loved so—ropa vieja and arroz con fri-joles, whose very scent awoke in him the memory of sweat-ing flesh, rumbas, street talk and sunshine that were part of his every day in his first homeland. On New Year's eve, his mother made Imperial Rice, with chunks of pork, ham, chicken and fish, just as she had in Cuba, in the days when the house they had inhabited was three times as small and so rickety that if you landed on the wrong floorboard, the whole place might have collapsed.

In the U.S. very little changed, except his parents' pride, which only grew with time—pride in country, pride in fam-ily, pride in their son. His parents worked just as hard and expected just as little.

After dinner, Hector's father enjoyed watching television—reruns of 70s shows like *All in the Family*, his face frozen into a smile as if those inside the TV set had conspired to give him just what he needed, as if he understood any of it. Hector would actually grit his teeth watching him. Although Hector loved his father, who was a good man, Hector also thought him a fool and saw himself as the one in his family who really knew the score and understood the ways of the world. He was convinced of this despite the fact that his parents had put up with a lot from him.

As a youth he had been a mediocre student with no in-centive whatsoever to improve himself intellectually. The re-port cards brought home included few accolades, although his ever-supportive mother never failed to point out, "Look, he passed here," as if that had been a major accomplishment. It was not that he lacked intelligence so much as the motivation to learn what he simply was not interested in learning. In class all he felt was a ticking anxiety, like a giant, unseen metronome inside him.

He was always the one sitting in back, legs splayed, fidgeting with something on the desk, usually a pen, that became a cell phone soon as the bell rang that he twirled and twirled, while always wearing that droopy-eyed look that frustrated his teachers but turned the girls on. There were only scattered impressions he took from his educational experience—the legs of Matilde Johnson, the eyes of Janet Hemmings, the bosom of Maria Conchita Sanchez-Hererra, and only one teacher's words.

One day, while handing back the folded blue composition booklet that hid the C-minus he had garnered on his half-finished essay on The American Constitution, his history teacher Mrs. Anderson said to him, "Hector Lopez-Garcia, I hope you learn to do something useful outside this classroom, something that actually excites you because certainly history is not your thing." What she meant of course was that he should start thinking about what he wanted to do with his life. Until Mrs. Anderson said what she did to him, it had not occurred to Hector to think at all about his future.

Mrs. Anderson's advice stayed with him. What could a young man like himself do to get ahead? What did he want to do? He began to mull these questions over in his mind, like newfound objects whose usefulness he could not fathom, and, at first they caused him distress. For who was he, besides a North American Cuban son, a jodido, tied to two Cubanos who knew very little beyond family love and belief in country. Everything seemed so simple to them, so black and white. Where was their hunger for anything save the Afro-Cuban jazz that they sought out like addicts on the radio dial that might as well have been to them the greatest gift on earth.

On Sunday afternoons, his parents went through their rituals of self-assertion, asserting to themselves and to Hector, who they were as individuals as they danced mambos and rumbas together while listening to WBCB, and with their riveting sense of patience and timing, showed off what it meant to be Cuban. His mother's hips, which Hector's small legs had straddled so often as a boy, and on which her left elbow often rested whenever she was wielding a spoon or ladle while conjuring some recipe in the kitchen, jerked and flipped at the same rate as his father's feet, which were fantastically nimble, even when he danced in house slippers. From the knees down his father was like a magician.

His mother's hazel eyes fixed on her father's black eyes, sometimes raking the long dimple down one cheek, while his father's mischievous glance kept slipping across his wife's sensual thighs. When Juan did a rumba, he pulled out his red, party hanky, twirling it in the air and flipping it between his legs, then used it to encircle Rosa's hips. His brown hand with its dirt-rimmed fingernails snapped the raised flag of passion, of music, of dance. Then she turned, seeming to wave him off with both hands, wearing such a smile. Hector had witnessed this since he was a kid, always thinking they were the most ridiculous and amazing couple in the entire universe.

The love that Hector's parents had for each other and for

the United States of America, he himself had for nothing, and for a while in his young adulthood this filled him with bitterness. He longed to find something of value for himself. He accepted he had not been a good student and that he had additionally been a bit irresponsible twice crashing the family car, a baby blue 1963 Buick Riviera that was his father's pride. Still, despite all this fucking up, as soon as he could, Hector did what he knew he should, made an attempt to become his own man, and upon his high school graduation, moved out of his parents' house. He began changing his ways, behaving like a young man striking out into the world, returning home only occasionally, as a good son does to prove his faithfulness.

And still he had no clue what he would do. Certainly, Hector knew what he did not want. Despite the fact that Hector's father had mentioned the trades many times to him over the years and was himself a well-respected mechanic who ran a popular shop with his brother and cousin, Hector himself had no such inclination. The mere idea of spending his days peering into the hood of a car, getting greasy, or wheeling under vehicles staring up at their filthy metallic underbellies, repulsed him. If he was sure of one thing, it was that this kind of life was not for him. Every time his father pressed him to come to the shop, to learn "the tools of the trade," his stomach actually churned.

Fortunately, his mother always came to his defense. "My son will find his own way," she declared proudly to relatives and friends, whenever they came to dinner and inquired in the third person about the young man sitting sullenly at one end of the table, the good-looking son, the only child and pride of the family.

In order to pay for his new place, Hector got busy mowing lawns, and helping a friend of his father move furniture for a month, and he got additional part-time work selling tickets and popcorn at a movie theater. Then somebody told him he could make good bucks working as a bouncer at a nightclub in the city, so he tried that.

Club Havana was known for hosting decent Afro-Cuban jazz bands. There was dancing Thursdays through Sundays, and Sunday afternoons, the management handed out free cigars. Hector became close to the house band, whose rhythm section inspired him. He thought the drummer Manny was off the charts. Completely bald, he wore leather bands that cinched his pump wrists as if to keep his hands from flying off his body whenever he played fast and furious.

A skinny, short guy played bongos, and a drunk worked the tumbadoras. Jorge, Carlos and Javier, all dapper guys, played horns. As if to distinguish themselves, one wore a mustache; another, a hat; and the other, wire rimmed glasses. Additionally, there was a young Juilliard graduate on piano, a white-haired Cubano on flute, and a sax player who looked exactly like Lester Young. One afternoon, before their gig, Manny and Hector got to talking, and Hector started messing around on the tumbadoras, imitating what he had so often seen and heard. Manny raised his eyebrows and cocked his head. He liked this kid, and his sound was good.

"Why don't you come hang with us this weekend. A few

of us like to jam at Columbus Circle. Come along and let's see how you work those congas in a group."

Over the course of the summer, Hector hung out in the park. It was there he met the slender Camila whose hips never ceased moving in his direction. It was there he developed his confidence and abilities playing a variety of drums, listening, following and picking up tunes from the Cuban ensemble. But his hands were magnetized to the tumbadora. He could not get enough of it. This was his instrument.

All his life, he had heard the names, "Tanga," "Mario Bauzá," "Tito Puente," and "Chano Pozo," who was his idol. Now he was getting the details, answers to questions about the music, the other side of what his parents had taught him. He was amazed at all he knew and did not know.

He knew for example that in 1943, it was Mario Bauzá, founder and director of Machito & His Afro-Cuban Orchestra, who, with a composition called "Tanga," merged traditional Afro-Cuban rhythms with the fresh harmonies of jazz, evolving a new genre, Afro-Cuban jazz. He did not know that this idea of jazz improvisation over intense Afro-Cuban rhythms would one day fuel Miles Davis's own musical experiments.

After "Tanga," came "Manteca" and "Tin Tin Deo," both of which were popularized by a brief collaboration between the great Dizzy Gillespie and the crazy, mad, brilliant drummer Chano Pozo. "Tanga," "Manteca," "Cubop City," and other great numbers, became part of Hector's repertoire. He was always with the group, always learning, quickly outshining his other compadre on the tumbadoras, who was always late for gigs, often sloppy drunk. Hector now had his own set of three congas; he was reliable when it came to music; he was good. Still, it came as a surprise when Manny invited him to join the group.

He was not even 19 and a professional musician. Hector was on top of the world. He was now ready to make the call home that he had been waiting to make and had been looking forward to making, the call that would explain his long absence from the family, that would explain where he had been. It was time to tell his parents who he was and to invite them to come hear him play.

His father's voice sounded strange to him from the first. "Your mother is sick, viejo. You need to come home. You need to come home and pay your respects," his father said to him, speaking in a hoarse whisper.

"Pa, how can I do that. We play tonight through Sunday. Please, give mama a big hug for me. She will understand. When she gets well, you can both come and see me play. Pa, I'm doing so good. Aren't you happy for me?"

"Son, your mother had a stroke three days ago. She is still in the hospital." Only then did those direct words of truth set him straight about the reality of the situation, and once he knew where she was, Hector was off and running, his mind, a whirr. He was not even sure of what he had just heard, just that he had to go.

"I will be back," he told someone while running out the doors of Club Havana.

The sun struck his eyes cruelly, and for a moment, he felt he had not seen sun in ages, had become a stranger to it, and had perhaps without realizing it, wilted a little inside from its lack of care. This was not a thought exactly, but a deeper awareness, that along with the fear that was growing inside him about his mother's condition, began chipping at his sense of grandness, the feeling he had been cultivating so long that he had wanted to share. He hopped a cab to Grand Central, and from there, a train to Norwalk, then a bus to Norwalk Hospital.

A quivering sense of trepidation overcame him as he rounded the corner to his mother's hospital room. What would he find? What would he say to her? Was this his mother, pale and still as he had never seen her, tubes spilling out of her mouth, her face contorted, one arm bent and frozen, eyes partially open, so many machines surrounding her? Only a few months ago she had been cooking and dancing, weaving her dream of happiness around him and his father. Surely this here now was a bad dream, nothing more.

"Mama. Mamacita." He grabbed one of her cramped hands with the perennially chipped nail polish. Her hand was warm. Did he sense a twitch of recognition in her eyes? The constant, hoarse breath of the machines frightened him. What if the machines stopped?

"Mama? Can you hear me? Mama, please wake up. This is Hector, your son. I am playing music now, tumbadoras." Just as his voice rose with pride, it broke and he collapsed weeping into his mother's hand, the hand that had cooked for him, adored and nurtured him all his life.

"Mama, listen to me. I am good. I am in a group. Can you hear me? Please nod, do something." She was stiff, warm still, but completely out of it. He glanced at a clock ticking loudly overhead and saw that it was time for him to go. But first he would call his father, let him know he had come, had been there. He picked up the receiver from the phone on the nightstand and called his father's house. The phone rang and rang. Finally his Tio Luis, his father's brother, picked it up. "It's me, Tio. I am here at the hospital with mama. I just wanted papa to know."

"Hombre, get off the phone. There is something wrong with your father. He just had some kind of attack. Your mother's absence, her condition, it's just too much for him. I have to call an ambulance."

His beloved father suffered a heart attack, one from which he did not recover, passing away that very night, on the eve of Hector launching his career and, as if that irony were not enough, almost one week to the day after his father's funeral, his mother came to.

She recovered physically, although most of her memory was gone, names and a colorful past eradicated, all but her ability to cook. The recipes she knew were inextricable, in her blood. The strangest thing was she never inquired about her deceased husband. One sensed that a part of her knew and still she could not bear to actually hear the truth, so, out of kindness, nobody told her directly.

She knew of course from that sensing place that was still very much alive inside her that Hector was her son, and always cast him a maternal, appreciative glance, but she rarely spoke. The stroke had left her placid, kind and capable to a degree, but void of all the particularities of her former person. Still, it was enough for Hector, for everybody. After all, she was still here, still alive, still Rosa.

Little by little she came back, moving slowly through the days. Hector moved back to the house to be with her with his woman Camila, and Rosa continued to cook for the family. Her eyes no longer beheld the world with their enthusiastic luster, for they had lost their unique object, but because there was no exact memory of the loss, she still did what she could, loving in whatever ways she had available to her those who surrounded her. It was the way of women in her world.

One Sunday, after one of Rosa's amazing Cuban repasts, when Hector figured his mother was well enough, he asked his uncle to bring her to the club to hear him play.

At the club, his Uncle Luis and mother sat together, he dressed all in white, she in her best red and black dress and well-worn pumps. Before beginning the set, Hector leaned toward a microphone and said, "I dedicate this to my dear mother Rosa Lopez-Garcia, who is here in the audience, and to my father, Juan Lopez-Garcia, to you papi." His eyes raised to heaven and he pointed up with one hand. "This is for you."

The band launched with "Tanga," and Hector, full of confidence, strutted his strong, mature hands firmly and proudly across the stretched skin of time of his instrument— toom, toom, toom, toom-toom—while his eyes fixed on his mother's aging brow and brimming glance and perpetual smile of hope, and soon she began applauding silently and her hips began shifting slightly in her seat as together with the band, Hector brought the audience home.

Don't Threaten Me With Love, Baby

Chantal Doolittle wasn't like anybody else she knew. Who else, for example, would stand transfixed before a record player or stereo, still as stone while listening to music—not merely attending to it—her very cells taking in the song, calculating and absorbing. "That girl is special," Nana Esther always said.

When she was a kid and Motown was the thing, Chan would sing Marvin Gaye's tunes to her grandmother in their high ceilinged apartment, where, more often than not it was soul music, the harmonizing voices of The Four Tops, The Temptations, The Supremes, drifting in from the surrounding windows and disappearing into the sky that was perennially a washed out gray, as if there was an invisible flag always at half mast, hanging outside heaven. From the time she was five or six, all Chan had to do was hear a song once and she would know it. She knew all the Motown tunes word for word, and sang them right on key, perfectly, which is why Nana Esther dubbed her, "my little songbird."

Of course there was nothing little about Chantal, but being her grandmother's one and only, she was "a little one" to her. Chantal was tall, big for her age, and when she developed as a young woman, busty too. She stood out even before she opened her mouth, due to her attitude. Her nana had taught her to be "confident as a man," and she had seemingly no fear in her. Chantal's parents had died when she was barely two, and in an attempt to reverse the shock of destiny, Nana Esther had raised her to believe anything at all was possible, that whatever life shelled out in the way of obstacles or hardship would be just temporary on the way to something grander.

You would have thought those two lived at The Ritz, the way they carried on at home, Nana Esther making a big to-do even about drawing drapes, turning everything into a ritual. "Too much sun, darlin'?"

"Not enough, my lady."

Nana Esther had a blue rose china tea set some relative had foisted on her that she was as proud of as a million dollar inheritance, and every afternoon at three, they had their tea. Nana Esther held her teacup to pursed lips, pinkie up, and nibbled on saltines like a little mouse, barely making a sound. "Pinkie up, Chan. This is how they do it," trying to prep Chan for that future time when she would be imbibing with high society.

In reality, the apartment they inhabited, like so many others in Harlem at the time, had plumbing problems the landlord never bothered to fix, and vermin too. Once, Nana Esther nearly passed out after finding a rat napping on the nest of her nighties in a drawer. Chantal got it out, pulling out all the drawers and flipping an antique porcelain lamp as she ran it out of their apartment. A Greek neighbor chased it out of the building with a broom, his family members yelling after him, "Fiye, fiye," which means, "go away." Into an alley that rat went, no doubt to continue procreating. There were more rats and roaches in that section of Washington Heights, along 155th street bordering Harlem, than there were people.

In the 60s and 70s, Harlem was not such a pretty place, certainly not as seen through news on TV and certainly not in the hood, where crime and drugs proliferated. Knowing Chan's fate might easily follow that of her own daughter and son-in-law, both of whom had succumbed to heroin and died of overdoses, Nana Esther kept a tight rein on Chan, long as she could.

Like the Calathea plants that grew in the living room, Nana Esther herself needed little sunlight and preferred the indoors. Having been afflicted with polio as a youth, she had used the help of a cane, far back as Chan could remember. Sundays, Chan and Nana Esther walked down the street to St. Thomas's Church arm-in-arm, Nana Esther, only then without a cane, in her big broad-rimmed red hat and black dress with a red and white trim and red flats to match, and Chan in her Sunday best white crinoline dress, with white cotton socks and black patent leather shoes. The two of them went off to church faithfully until one Sunday, when Chan was about 12, and Nana Esther announced she was too old and too tired to "to hear the sermons of a lecher." It was Father Rob she was referring to, the same priest that a teenager in their parish, a delicate boy with down-turned eyes, had accused of being a molester.

Anybody who wanted to see Nana Esther came to her. She had "an apartment to keep and a child to raise and that's enough for anybody my age." Sundays after service, the church folk came over, bearing steaming dishes of black eyed peas, fried chicken, greens and cornbread, their kids and grandkids in tow so they could fraternize with Chan, who could have cared less about their company. Most of the time, Chan hung in a corner, staring at the brats with that sideways, suspicious glance of hers, putting up with the noise and confusion like some old lady. Once, when she was stretched out on the couch, polishing off a barbequed chicken wing, Leon Fisher threw himself on her and tried to tongue-kiss her. Chan slapped him so hard, the boy wouldn't stop bawling, so his embarrassed mother and grandmother, grabbed a hold of their dish of half-eaten ham hocks, and took off, shoving Leon out the door first.

That sort of thing didn't ruffle Nana Esther at all. She had taught Chan to be independent, and a slap is what that boy deserved. She knew Chan wasn't anti-social, merely willful. Nobody could force her to do anything or tell her what to do. "Long as she stays out of trouble." But Nana Esther knew better about that too, for pride and strength in a girl or woman always lead to trouble.

As a girl, Chan attended P.S. 186, a fine-looking Renaissance-style building on 145th Street, off Broadway, where one of Nana Esther's best friends Ruth taught Math, and where Chan was always getting sent to the principal's office for back talking in class, or fighting with boys at recess. Seemed like every other week she had to stay after school to write do's and don'ts on the chalkboard. A few years after Chan graduated, P.S. 186 closed down, becoming just another tombstone in Harlem.

For a long time, Nana Esther dreamed of seeing Chan go off to St. Mary's dressed in a clean white pressed blouse, plaid jumper, green bow tie and saddle shoes, sure that nuns would have inspired in her a love of books, settled her down, but the truth was, going to private school wouldn't have made a difference. Chan would have resisted that too, for all authority ever aims to do is to tell you how to behave and bend you to its truth.

Whenever she'd catch Chan just staring out the window, Nana Esther would say, "There's nothing out there but trouble, with a capital T. I don't want or need none of it," as if repeating that enough, she might get the child to believe it too. She knew there would come a time when there would be nothing she could do to protect Chan, nothing at all.

Everything that had to do with Chan—her school photos, drawings, report cards, birth certificate—Nana Esther squirreled away neatly in white boxes that filled most of the space of the bureaus in her boudoir. Those keepsakes were all Nana Esther had to pass on, that and the far out records that sat next to the Emerson HiFi that was Chan's favorite companion, in the living room.

It was on that Emerson that Nana Esther played for Chan

all the music she herself had grown up listening to—the music of Charlie Parker, Lester Young, Dizzy Gillespie, and most especially, the original songbird herself, Lady Day. For a long time, jazz was the magic that kept Chan at home, the glue that kept grandmother and granddaughter together—until another kind of magic came along.

When Chan was 20, trying to turn a fresh page on her life, straightening herself out in a nut farm in Litchfield, she discovered through a friend, that Lady Day had passed away on July 17, 1959, the day before her own birth. Years after she stopped using, after she herself had become a professional, performing on Broadway, she still nurtured the notion, bred in that time, that she herself had been Lady Day in another life.

It wasn't just that they were both contraltos, had both grown up poor, raised by proud, self-sacrificing women—Billie, by her mother, and Chan, her grandmother. Or that, like Billie, Chan had run into trouble as a young girl, and had whored around, carrying her head high through the losses of loves, men and women alike that had filtered through her life like sand, bearing everything like a trooper—again, like Billie. It was that she felt they shared the same essence, the same heart, the truest bond.

Whenever she told her story in Narcotics Anonymous, Chan always made a point of letting people know her original intention getting on the stuff had never been to escape life or get out of it, but the opposite. Chan had imagined the magic powder would take her deeper into the music she loved, so she could understand it from the inside out, like so many others before her, like the great artists she loved had. She had hoped "the evil dust," as Nana Esther called it, would lift her up like a great blues or jazz song.

"Far back as I can remember, music was the one thing I knew gave me complete satisfaction and inner calm. I loved Billie Holiday's tunes, especially, and wanted to sing like her, out of my gut and heart, always en point." She would look around the room to make sure everybody understood her reference, being then a woman of the world, having been to a white nut farm, where she had acquired a different kind of articulation among rich white folk recovering from mental issues and addiction, like her.

"I took my first snort at 15 out in Harlem. Before gentrification, it was a place that reeked of style and the great music that was its heritage. Music was everywhere, surmounting even the poverty and problems.

"I was still in junior high when I got my first real exposure outside a bar called Paris Blues. I was just hanging out, you know, too young to be inside, singing along with whatever was sifting out into the street, picking up whatever I could, and this dude with a maroon suit and hat passing by, says to me. 'Little girl, you sure can sing.' So I kept it up, showing off a little, knowing I had an audience. He watched me, slanty-eyed, nodding his head, and said, 'You know what all the great singers and musicians do to hear a tune right, to really get in the groove, right?' I said, 'No, sir.' And so he took out this little white packet and started wagging it in front of me, while flashing this big gold-toothed grin at me. So, I snatched that little bag and took off with it. I guess he didn't figure what a good runner I was too."

The story of a life is the story of two or three defining incidents, and that was one for Chan, along with the routine of listening to Nana Esther's jazz records as a kid. Although she did not ingest that bag for months, hiding it under her pillow instead like something to dream on, the things that came only a couple of years after that meeting, the hooking and nastiness, the dimming of song and music itself, rather than its amplification, drove Chan into the deepest darkest despair and to the one place she had never imagined she would land—jail.

Lucky for her, Chan wasn't found with stuff directly on her when everybody at Cecil's party in the Village got arrested, or she might have done real time. Oh but the humiliation, standing in a courtroom, facing her nana, the only judge she cared about, in a mini skirt and tank top, no less. Her nana had never even seen her dressed like that either.

For the first time in years, as Nana Esther leaned forward in her seat, right hand with her cane hooked around her wrist, firm on the back of the pew in front of her, as if she might actually keel over, Chan could see how gray and bent her grandmother had gotten. Nana Esther looked down and shook her head sadly, unable or unwilling to believe what had become of her "little songbird." What would Nana Esther have done, Chan wondered, had she actually known Chan had been one of those whores kicked out of a Grand Central Station bathroom after being caught bird-bathing at a sink? That alone would have surely killed her.

They were all lucky that day—Cecil, to have been caught with less than four ounces on him, and everybody else because Jamal had split with most of the shit before the police got there, and Chantal and the other girl, for not having been arrested and booked on charges before then.

Chan did 30 days in jail, and 30 more of community service, then, following the advice of a social worker, started seeing a shrink. Dr. Freud, Chan called him, asked a lot of silly questions like, what did you dream about last night?— as if that had anything to do with reality. Then her nana got a stroke and Chan went back to living with her, while still finishing up what she called her "double time," helping out at a soup kitchen.

Chan had left home and school at 15, high on drugs and hungry to experience life, abandoning her grandmother just to keep her from seeing what she was up to, hopping from place to place and sleeping around randomly. Sometimes she sang with buddies on the streets and in parks for a little cash. She had always loved singing. But of course, if you are a young woman on your own, when times get hard, you do what you must to get by, and Chan had experienced everything.

Back in the apartment with her nana, Chan felt like a child again, with all the unspoken longing of an orphan to feel rooted to someone or something, and on top of that the stress of toxins still in her system from years abusing her body. She was back in that place that had once been home, and safe, but she was no longer innocent, no longer the person that had once believed there was only good to be found out there, only adventure.

Chan began to cop again, a little here and there, just

to deal with her bad feelings, anxiety about the future and fear of losing the one person she knew truly loved her. Although she was no longer hanging with the druggies, pimps, alkies and hookers that made up her street family, her past life haunted her, even as night after night, she sat with her grandmother, watching episodes of *All in the Family, Sanford and Son*, and *Good Times*, Nana Esther, drowsy with age and illness, and Chan, in that vague high place that is akin to nowhere. Instead of laughing openly as she used to, all Nana Esther had the energy to do then was tsk-tsk at what was funny, and what was in poor taste. It was all the same now. Their exchanges turned mostly wordless and sad, infused with an awareness of time gone by, and inevitabilities, perhaps. Then, overnight, as if knowing her job with Chan was done and there was no more she could do, Nana Esther passed away in her sleep.

More than loss, at first, Chan felt regret. There had been no time for promises or apologies. What would she have promised anyway—that she would never use again? That would have been false. Unspoken words and long silences had come between them over the years, but lies—never. What was the use of wishing things had turned out differently? The only thing Chan knew now certainly, was that in death, Nana Esther could see her every move. Whatever she had not known about Chan before, she now most certainly knew.

No longer was there any veil of distance or absence between them as there had been when she was a teenager off on her own, messing up. Of course she hadn't thought then she was running away from anything, only to life. And still, anytime she stood barefoot on a corner in her candy striped bellbottoms and leather vest, panhandling, whenever she sang soul numbers with brothers in a park, or turned out a jazz song, whenever she sat on a stoop or bench gazing at the sky beyond the rooftops of buildings that seemed as far away and unreachable as the sun, all she thought of then was the music she loved and how she might live in it. She had a dream of performing one day at Small's.

She remembered one time, actually catching a jazz concert at the Apollo. It was 1975 and she was that intense kid craning her neck so far forward to get a close look at the musicians, that it was sore for days. Gerry Wiggins was on piano, Major Holley on bass, and Ed Thigpen, the greatest drummer in the world—at least the greatest she had ever heard—so good he had even played with Oscar Peterson— on drums. A young, brash Rebecca Parris, wearing a cool man's watch and headband, sang "Since I Fell For You," and Chan thought then, "I can do better."

She was only 16, and already knew what she wanted to do, and also that the life she was living would lead nowhere if she lingered in it too long. Had Nana Esther's spirit been watching over her then, she would have understood what the running was all for. She might still, now that she was everywhere, overseeing and judging.

It was because Chan knew Nana Esther would always be there in death, vigilant over her life, that there was no way Chan could keep using. She would have to stop, and she needed help doing it.

"Dr. Freud," she said, "Why couldn't I have been straight when she died? I wanna die."

"No," said Dr. Freud, "you don't want to die. You want to live, you just need help learning how."

Dr. Freud told her to get away from the Heights, the Village and Harlem. He said he knew of a special rehab that took in young, talented people like her. The woman who ran it was a friend.

"I don't have much more than a dime," Chan reminded him.

A while back, one of Johnny Carson's ex wives, who had spent time there for alcoholism, had bequeathed a scholarship for an "underprivileged person," what minorities were called then, and Chan fit the bill. Chan could feel Nana Esther smiling down on her even as she rode with Dr. Freud toward Country Hills, away from her life in New York, her old hangouts, friends and habits, so far away it might as well have been another country.

The German psychotherapist who ran Country Hills had studied under Dr. Jung himself and only took in young people in their 20s, most of whom were neurotic—although one or two had experienced psychotic breaks—all of whom had some unique talent. The interview with Chan took place in a posh study, with Dr. Wagner perched stiffly at the edge of a high-backed chair, her blue eyes cool and steady on Chan behind her wire rims. Chan just answered questions, never said a word about singing, so she was more than a little surprised when at the end of the interview, she was asked to move in, for once, without having to sell herself at all.

Country Hills was like no place Chan had ever been to and no institution she had ever heard of, mostly because there were no bars and few rules. The main house, where Dr. Wagner, the females and a nurse lived, was a mansion, pure and simple, with ivy running up its brick walls, a marble entranceway and a view of rolling hills out back. A handful of males and a peer counselor lived in a nice white clapboard house a little further down the road; there was a residence for therapists too; and a garden in which lettuce, tomatoes, cucumbers, squash and the like grew, and a pond in which you could dip, nights when it got hot. There were no more than a dozen residents at Country Hills, and each was a character.

There was a manic depressive ex-therapist from Baton Rouge, once incredibly wealthy, who had gambled his money away while on a manic high; a suicidal actress/model who hated her beautiful body; a schizophrenic painter who could now only draw like a child; a sculptor who only created phallic shapes; a dyke poet recovering from alcoholism; a reggae drummer who had tried to run his car off a bridge; and a depressed dancer with an eating disorder.

These white, clean-cut grownup kids from well-to-do families looked for the most part like they had never seen daylight, and surely had never suffered physical deprivation; they had all attended or graduated college or some famous arts institute, yet rarely mentioned the world beyond Country Hills. It occurred to Chan they were more likely to associate the word, raid, with a bug spray than a drug bust. None had ever even met a hipster. And here was Chan, with a pick set defiantly in her Afro, carrying inside

her a well of stories and notes, Chan who had never graduated high school, but who knew the ways of the street inside
out, who had once even protested the Vietnam war that was
short-shifting blacks.

Chan listened to the stories of her peers at Country Hills,
intrigued by their vocabulary, and found that their travails
about not having enough money or parental attention or
friends, distracted her from her own recollections. She did
not mention that outside of the world of music, she herself
had few memories from her childhood to rely on. She had
only ever seen one faded photo of her parents—he, wearing a turtleneck and shades, she, too much mascara—that
her grandmother had framed and placed in the living room.
Outside of that, Chan did not even have parental voices to
remember.

Nana Esther had always been reticent and vague regard-
ing Chan's parents. Chan only knew they had met in Central
Park, and from that moment on, never once separated, and
that they had died only weeks apart. At one point Chan had
believed her Puerto Rican father was special, having taken
her mother's last name, only to learn later it was customary
in Latin America for a family to append the maternal sur-
name at the end. Doolittle was her grandmother's last name
and her mother's.

How often had Chan stared into her parents' eyes in that
photo, asking them why they had done what they had, de-
parting so soon, abandoning her, trying to pry out of their
façades some shred of story linked to her own life? How often had she resented their slight smirks and blank stares that

told her nothing? While those at Country Hills with whom she sat in groups had plenty to relay about their growing up years, she herself had no history to share, no place to claim outside of the apartment she had grown up in, nothing but the music—and how would they understand that? She began to wish she herself had suffered the parental punishments, abuse and neglect the others bemoaned in group therapy. At least then she would have had something to say.

It amazed Chan how fascinated her fellow residents were with themselves, how at home they felt exposing their innermost secrets and lives, personal experiences she herself would have never thought to divulge. That had never been her style, or the style of anybody she knew, although listening took her mind away from guilt feelings about losing the one person in life she had trusted, who was now gone, who she could not dwell on without tears and would therefore never mention, certainly not to a group. Unlike her friends at Country Hills, Chan did not consider tears a public province. They were meant to be kept private, released only in solitude.

Lucky for her, the counselors and residents at Country Hills mostly let her have her silence, a silence Chan cultivated and wore like a mask between her real business and that of her peers. For a while, even the two therapists that moderated the group sessions did not pierce it.

They might have had enough to deal with, monitoring Bonita's inappropriate, often outrageous interjections. While the others ruminated on their pasts, Bonita doodled compulsively, her scraggly hair dangling over her face, now and then bursting out with—"Oh, you're just saying that," or, "Liar!" or, "You *do* like her." A child's voice, she was also the chorus and truth teller in the group.

The first man Chan ever saw weep was Vince, who claimed his family had disowned him due to his love affair with an older, married woman, someone his family found abhorrent. But Chan, who watched and listened intently, could tell his wooden mask and folded hands that kept his wrists from going fey were just hiding the obvious—he was gay. More often than not, it was Sheila, the dancer, who wept disconsolately because her mother, a Hollywood actress, had not bothered either to call or visit the entire year Shiela had been at the Hills. The ideal stay at Country Hills, according to Dr. Wagner, was one to three years, which Chan determined early on wasn't going to happen with her, no way.

The problems of her friends seemed surreal to Chan. Not one had ever seen a person die or even lost a family member. She couldn't imagine how they would have reacted to her own sagas of abortions and ODs. She had seen so many blue-faced friends foaming at the mouth sprawled in mattresses and bathroom floors with needles sticking out of their arms, legs and feet, she could have wallpapered a room with their names and faces, all of which were impaled in her. No amount of lovely scenery or childlike reminiscences could eradicate that.

The group therapy process, which took place most afternoons in a downstairs salon of the main house, and in a second floor room of the males' dorm, struck Chan as somewhat absurd, even bizarre. There was for example that session in the large white-painted room in the clapboard house when they were each asked to strike a stack of stripped mattresses with blue foam bats while yelling out the name of an abuser. Chan demurred. Most of the folks she had grown up with spent their energy trying to hold back rage lest they kill somebody. But this group couldn't get their anger out. For a moment or two, Chan debated asking the therapist in charge for a real bat so she could go to town on those mattresses, but in the end decided to indulge instead in a little fantasy of feathers flying and her cohorts laughing up a storm in between spasms of shocked delight. Chan began to feel that what the rest of the world called madness was in fact a privilege of the rich, a lucky few. The poor couldn't afford it. It took up too much time, too much self-involvement.

Mornings, the residents had duties like cleaning the main house, scraping and painting its walls, preparing meals, and learning how to make lamps in a shed. Chan volunteered in the kitchen and learned how to make vegetarian meals, even fried zucchini blossoms.

So little was expected to heal from life's wounds. All you have to do is learn to cry and to cook, thought Chan. Well, it was a beginning, something to store inside, along with the music. Chan was never moved to sing while at Country Hills, in between all the things there were to do.

Dr. Wagner, who was very progressive, encouraged the residents to have relationships with one another, so they could explore them in groups. Chan didn't mind the relationship part, but talk about them? There was no way she was going to do that. But you know the saying—Never say never. It's a given if you stick two addicts in the same bedroom, then send them off together to AA meetings, that they are going to hit on one another. That was Chan's first mistake—sleeping with Jackie, the poet. Second mistake was sleeping with Paul, the ex-shrink from Florida, and third was thinking that wasn't going to cause a ruckus in group.

So she slept a couple of times with each of them. Why were they so freaked out to find out about the other? Wasn't that what they were supposed to do—have sex? Connect? What had each of them thought, that she was going to marry them?

Chan could have let the whole thing slide, put up with Paul going on about how sleeping with Chan had stirred up old feelings of anger about his mother's betrayal of his father, and Jackie's complaints about feeling so deceived and used. Who were these people talking about? Certainly not her. But the therapists thought this was a good time to penetrate Chan, get her to account.

They couldn't get a word out of Chan during sessions, so they started playing games, literally—the smiley faced Mary, who wore a long braid and always dressed in white—maybe so folks would confuse her with Florence Nightingale; and stoic Mark, who, when Chan had only been there three weeks, had taken the actress/model Alice back to her Park Avenue apartment so she could close it down, Mark who had been the one she had asked to make a sandwich for her while she gathered some things into a box in the living room and who found only open windows when he returned, as Alice had leapt 17 stories; Mark, who had stood by, ashen-faced, while an austere and handsome Chilean psychiatrist reported what had happened to the group. All the residents wept and imagined Alice, the most beautiful angel, flying over the skyline to a better destiny somewhere. Dr. Wagner was in Germany and Chan and the others held a candlelight vigil with her when she returned, commemorating the first death that had touched all of them together.

One time, each resident was asked to sit at the center of a circle alone and imagine what kind of fruit they felt like. When it came to Chan's turn, she said—avocado. The two therapists looked at one another like she had said something significant.

"Is it because an avocado is soft on the outside, but hard inside," started Mary.

"No," replied Chan, "it's because I like the damn fruit."

"Do you feel threatened, Chan?" inquired Mark.

"No, I don't feel threatened. Nobody's trying to sell me drugs or rape me, so, no, I don't feel threatened. What's up?"

"Maybe it's because you come from, well, different roots," said Mary. Again, the two counselors locked eyes, confirming they were on the verge of something deep and real.

"Maybe it's because of your upbringing, on the street. Do you feel threatened by love, Chan?"

She felt a hot rush of embarrassment and anger and for once vented what she was thinking—"If I did feel love, I'd be singing." With that, she stood, pulled her pick out of her back pocket, affixed it into her 'fro, and strutted to the area outside the kitchen, next to the green garbage bin, the only place you were allowed to smoke, and had herself a few.

She was so pissed off, her eyes burned. It was one thing

to watch the charade, and quite another to get caught in its spokes. She knew these professional helpers were well-meaning, and she was "the defiant one," what they had nicknamed her. But what were they trying to get her to do? And what, really, did she want to change about herself? And how long did she want to sit under the spell of this faux reality and pretty scenery?

A remembrance of difference coursed through her then. She must have been in the 5th grade and came home looking like a sad puppy, her nana said. Chan explained: "I tried to talk about jazz in Current Events class today, and Miss May shut me up, said it's not current."

"Not current?! It's as current as the day, as the skyline, the very street we live on. Why, jazz brought us up. What is that crazy woman talking about? What are they teaching you in school anyway?"

"Two plus two is four, and I already got that."

"Humph."

It was time to throw open the closet doors, far as jazz was concerned, thought Chan, time to throw them wide open. She realized she was not the only one whose life had been on hold at Country Hills. It was the nature of where they were—an emotional halfway house. She had not been able to sing while there, but Vince had not played drums, and Jackie had not written poems either. They had hung in mid air for months, in limbo, their lives on pause together. But it was time to go now. She was not regrouping with them, but internally, and she was ready to move on.

She had developed her ability to listen at Country Hills,

taking in the stories of her peers, a different kind of music, dissonant and unfamiliar. For a while, it had erased everything she knew and believed in. She was heading back to the city, back to the place of her birth, and her love of music and singing. Now, clean, New York was no longer a city to fear, but a wide, open space filled with notes, like her own interior.

Chan was being taken somewhere. Her eyes fixed on the back of the driver's head, his long, unruly, curly black hair that brought to mind foreign places she had never even visited but somehow recalled just from living. Chan watched his head tilt, listening.

A voice, much like Billie's, was singing, "Ain't Nobody's Business," and her lips followed the song—"but I'm going to do just as I want to anyway, and don't care just what people say." She could feel the words rising out of truth and fear and knowing in her. Only then did she realize, it was her own voice returning.

"Don't threaten me with love," is a quote attributed to Billie Holiday.

Like a Pigeon in the Park

"What a shame," people always said whenever they saw the two together, Jeremy and Jade. What a shame the beauty of the boy had escaped the girl, who had her mother's small oval face and father's prominent nose and small dark eyes that were filled with a peculiar, almost unnatural intensity. "Such a shame," relatives observed unabashedly at family gatherings. The remaining phrase that hung in air unspoken was, "that she isn't the beautiful one."

To herself in the mirror, Jade's own face and visage seemed fine, just a part of her, not even all that consequential. Didn't brains and character matter more? She was striking much in the way Zelda Fitzgerald had been—a beauty you could not capture in photographs, more in movement, gesture, articulation. Somewhere, not far from the small, provincial town where Jade lived, where people stared at you if you did not fit into a mold, there were people like her who were different and proud of their differences and she looked forward to meeting them one day. In the meantime, she understood life might have its challenges.

Growing up, challenges mostly had to do with her brother, who was two years older. Although Jade garnered high marks in school, not much was made of it so as not to embarrass Jeremy, who struggled with his grades. To her parents, aunt, uncle and cousins, it seemed a crime someone so good-looking should have to deal with anything that diminished him. Jeremy's struggle with his grades endowed him with an almost tragic aura and only served to make him more appealing in his vulnerability, so he was spoiled even more.

While Jade's A's were treated as B's, Jeremy's B's and even C's were treated as top grades. Once, at the dinner table, Jade wondered aloud to her parents—"Do you care that I'm an honor student?" Her mother responded by daintily scooping up a mouthful of lemon ice and placing it on her tongue as if to keep herself from uttering something inappropriate.

"Yes," her father said, "Of course, we know that," registering mainly impatience with his daughter whose constant questioning of everything rattled his nerves. He was always letting her know what he thought of her tendency toward curiosity—"Why do you always want to know why? Not everything is yours to know. Remember, curiosity…"

"Yes," Jade would say, "I know, dad. Curiosity killed the cat." Then she would roll her eyes at some unseen ally who witnessed her predicament, turn and leave the room.

It was as if her father, who rarely heard or understood her, wanted her to remain in a bubble of ordinariness. At the same time, her mother always refrained from contradicting him, making waves or even suggesting she thought differently from the "man of the house." They were so old-fashioned, so typical of the Midwestern town in which they had lived all their lives.

No matter what the actual circumstances, it was always Jeremy, the first born, the beauty, who got support and praise, and not just from his family—from everyone. Once, as a junior, he was selected to act in a play in which he had little more to do than kiss a girl, then turn to the audience smirking, but he brought the house down like a would-be star in his first production.

After graduating, Jere returned to their high school to perform with his pop/jazz group. Wearing jeans, a tight tee and expensive Maui Jim sunglasses their mother bought for him, he looked like a cross between James Dean and a young Chet Baker. Jere was facile on the horn, although his overconfidence and lack of discipline caused him to err in ways only a trained ear could detect. It made Jade wince at times.

He stood to the side, a short distance from the bass player and drummer, and when he was not blowing his horn, stroked and kissed it, a bit of business that kept attention on him, so at the end of the gig, the audience composed mainly of crushes and friends of the family, gave him a standing ovation. His parents, thrilled by his antics, applauded him mightily.

Psychologists say a child's ego is formed in the first year, and if all goes well then, no matter what damage may follow, the child will be able to shoulder it. It was thanks to her Uncle

Mel that Jade always felt buoyed by support, cared for, and thanks to him she found her passion early.

Shortly after Jade's coming into the world, Jade's mother found herself overwhelmed by post-partum depression and went to stay with her sister in Missouri. As Jade's father could only handle one child, Jade was sent to live with her Uncle Mel in New York. Mel was single, had never had a child, and delighted in his temporary charge for whom he bought not only a crib, but a playpen, placing overhead and within his niece's view, mobiles of colorful star shapes and laminated photos of movie stars and famous musicians he saw regularly in the city. Surely, thought Jade much later, these must have wooed her subconscious. And for nine months he played the music he loved, the best jazz and Broadway tunes he owned, for her.

At six, there was only one thing Jade knew she wanted to do, study music. Her parents resisted—she was too young and they did not want to indulge a mere phase. They were amused at the idea she merely wanted to emulate her brother. She was 10 when they finally relented, and then it was only because her piano classes coincided with Jeremy's horn lessons at Silvermine Music School. Her parents gave her permission to study piano—what else would a girl play? By the time she was 12, Jade was fluent in the standards most students take twice as long to learn and eager to try something new. After studying the crazy inventiveness of Bird and others on Youtube, she fixed on the alto sax.

No way, said her dad. Her parents were appalled and a little disturbed she would choose such a masculine instrument.

"What are you thinking? Where will that get you," her father said. But Jade kept pressing them. They finally bought her an alto figuring she could learn her instrument while keeping Jeremy company in the studio they built for him.

"Was that you?" Jade's mother sometimes inquired when she and Jere emerged from the studio after a session. "Was that you playing the sax so beautifully, or your brother, teaching you how?"

"Talent runs in the family," Jeremy said, flicking back a strand of his sister's hair, rubbing her cheek playfully with the back of a forefinger.

Encouraged by the stream of girls that never failed to flock to him after gigs, and by his own family's enthusiasm for all he did, Jeremy kept his sights on what he assumed was a kind of birthright—success in the music industry—so when it came time to go to college, he went to a local school close to home, so he could always come back to his studio to practice, to do what he was meant to do. He and Jade often hung out there jamming, sometimes with friends.

While Jere took everything for granted—from his parents to the love of his friends and sister, Jade herself took nothing for granted, working hard at odd jobs through high school, putting aside money so she could leave home and forge a real life after graduation. Then something happened that made all the difference to her.

Uncle Mel passed away leaving her his rent-controlled apartment on West 10th Street in New York. Jade was a senior then and Jeremy had not yet dropped out of college. This was the small square of freedom Jade needed that Uncle

Mel had always intended to give her, to nurture her potential and talent, having always been the one family member who believed in her. An apartment in New York's West Village was a dream come true, and Jade seized her opportunity.

In New York Jade felt like someone who mattered among others who, like her, were evolving their dreams and talents. Her small, cozy studio had a warm shag rug and a high ceiling that provided decent acoustics. A bookcase full of CDs and books divided the living room from her sleeping area. Sometimes she opened the back screen door and played to weepy trees that loomed over her back patio. She worked hard as a waitress and practiced long hours on her own, looking forward to the time when it would feel right to share her music.

What is a girl? She had asked herself that question so often when she lived at home. Away from home, she explored more relevant questions like, what makes an artist? The first part of her life had been full of limitations. Now it felt limitless, rife with possibilities to match her expectations.

One Sunday, unassumingly, almost as if she was catching her own self by surprise, Jade grabbed her instrument case and took the subway to the hottest spot she could think of in the city—Wall Street, where there was a revolution going on and therefore, where jazz belonged.

Positioning herself across from Zuccotti Park, Jade took out her alto, braced herself, one sneakered foot back against the wall of a bank, and played her "Prelude" for protesters across the way. This would be her spot Tuesdays and Sundays, her days off.

During the week, stockbrokers and other businesspeople strutted arrogantly by, as if vaguely insulted by Jade's intrusion, or rather, that of jazz, which they may have connected in some way to the protest movement in the park. Sporting a brown beret, vest and baggy jeans, Jade showed she had style, fitting in the diverse milieu where activists dressed like hippies and beatniks, reflecting other eras.

From the first, when Jade began playing in public, it seemed to her this was all she had ever done—perform for strangers, wooing them so they could not ignore her going by. Sometimes passersby not only paused to listen, they smiled at her. Sometimes they reached into pockets and handbags to toss a bill or two or change into her open case. This was an accomplishment in New York, where people's taste doesn't lie, where artists are expected to be both excellent and unique, and the question always asked is—who is great? Who besides Vi Redd, Candy Dulfer or Gigi Dryce could be that good? Greatness was a needle in a haystack, especially in New York.

One evening after her sidewalk gig, Jade decided to check out what was happening across the street. She came upon a young man behind a tent cycling fast on a stationary bike, a practical way to create energy and electricity in the park. Next to him, under a bright bulb, sat a young woman reading *Manifestoes of Surrealism*. Between her and the cyclist, on a chalkboard leaning against a tree were the names of people who would take turns cycling to keep up electricity. Just away, a young couple wearing dreds tousled affectionately while painting each other's faces with primitive designs. Sunset shed a warm, optimistic light on all these people that, like Jade, knew something beyond the ordinary and, like her, were happy in self-created worlds.

For the moment, Jade likened herself to a pigeon she saw perch on a sign that read, "Greed is not a family value," as if to parlay a message, but it took off as she approached. "Chicken," she called out. And somebody yelled back, "Don't worry, they always come back." Jade smiled to herself. Like those pigeons, she would alight with her music, depart, and return.

In public, she soon found she preferred wearing a façade, something to hide behind, so attention would remain on her music and not on her. On Sundays, which were especially crowded and busy, she wore a top hat and coat. The costume helped her stay focused, inside herself. As sunlight beat down on the round top of her hat, she could hear change jingling as it fell among the bills inside her open black case. People crowded close creating an encompassing shade and Jade closed her eyes to escape deeper into the music. She frowned, her eyelids pinching shut, her brow furrowing with concentration.

She closed her eyes against the brightness of the sun and the skyline, against too many people and their complicated lives of doubt and discontent, and blew her own version of jazz standards—"My Favorite Things," "Body and Soul," "Summertime," and "Georgia On My Mind." On the best days, as sun started to set and people began heading homeward, she spun out a most unearthly rendition of "Europa," tenderly enunciating the special language of her instrument so strangers going home could own it too as they faded into the distance.

Jade enjoyed the musical challenges, playing counter to

the music of people's voices, constant calls and chanting and assorted drums, all beating with the energy of a new movement. The fresh sounds inspired and stimulated her, encouraged her to stay true to herself and what she knew. Sometimes she collected decent money on her adventures, once as much as $240 in a single day. Sometimes people threw in business cards with their money and she kept them too.

One fourth of July weekend, after a killer shift at The Lemon Tree, where she worked, Jade decided to bypass her routine in the park and attend to other business. Relaxing on her studio love seat, she sorted through the cards she had collected. One read, "Sonny Jones," had a number, and nothing more. "Sonny," like Sonny Stitt and Sonny Rollins. Who would not like that name? So she tapped his number into her phone.

"What? Hello? Who is it?" The man's voice at the receiving end was harsh. Reception was static-y, so Jade hollered, "You gave me your card. I play Sundays at Zuccotti Park."

"What? Who is this? Wrong number, whoever you are. I don't have time for this," he said.

"Fucking occupier," she heard him say to someone just before the call went dead. Jade laughed to herself.

"First try, you luck out. Try again," she told herself. She would keep at it. The right person would come along eventually to help her branch out. It was just a matter of time. Jade put away the business cards and picked up a letter from Jere she had received a few days before, and stretching out so her legs hung over one armrest of the love seat, she re-read it.

"Dear Sis," it read. "I know it's been a while. I've been

meaning to write forever. It's different without you here. You're my sounding board." She skipped mundane paragraphs and went to the second page. "The trio broke up. You'll be surprised to learn it wasn't me, at least not really. Remember Dean? Big brown eyes, model Dean? We've been seeing each other, spending a lot of time in the studio because it's the one place where mom and dad never go. I mean it was our space. But of course I made the mistake of giving the guys a key. Anyway, to make a long story short, Dick and Charlie now know. They made it clear they don't want to be associated with or seen with a fag, so the group is over, done.

"I'm not blaming anybody. Dean and I are together and that's what matters to me. That and the fact I know you're cool with your brother being gay and want me to be happy. I'm definitely busted up about the trio, but the thing that worries me most is wondering whether Dick and Charlie will start spreading the word about me. I mean, what could I do to stop them? Nothing. Surprisingly, the fact there will be no more gigs bothers me less than being dragged out of the closet. I hope you're killing it in NYC. xoxox."

Slowly, Jade re-folded the letter and put it away. Jere was playing Russian Roulette having a same-sex affair in that place. She had not been all that surprised when he came out to her before going off to college, but straight, conservative Salem was no place to be of the closet. Under Obama, things had gotten better for gays, but that was not true everywhere in America. New York would be much better to Jere and Dean.

The following Sunday as Jade played her outdoor gig, a

crazy-eyed hipster with a goatee and a jacket with patches at the elbows caught her eye. He cocked his head in her direction as he listened, then suddenly clasped his forehead with one hand, swearing under his breath. The moment she stopped playing, he approached her. "Hey, I'm Sonny Jones. I apologize. It was you who called the other night, right?" She broke into a smile, "yeah."

"Oh, man, I couldn't hear you. I was at a party. I'm so sorry. You're outta sight. Did you study at Juilliard? Berklee?"

"Neither."

He couldn't get over the fact Jade was mostly self-taught. He checked her out—waif-like, crazy hair, and what an out-fit. "Kid, you've got IT, you know that. Tell me what you want to do. Let me buy you some coffee." He pulled out a wad of greasy bills almost impulsively. She gently pushed his hand with the money wad away, laughing nervously. What was he thinking? No doubt it was part of his schtick. She couldn't wait to hear what he had to tell her.

They settled for the nearest Starbucks and, as they sat with their drinks, Jade checked out his dirt-rimmed finger-nails and somber, fixed gaze. He leaned toward her shelling out promises, and she half-listened, another part of her al-ready knowing his words. Here was someone almost as hun-gry for success as she was. Greed in this case was good. She wanted to work with someone who cared that much about her music, who would fight for her. For a time anyway, Son-ny's greed would work for her. She shook his hand. "Get me the gigs. You'll get your share. Deal?"

"You bet, kid. I'm in."

Heading back to West 10th, Jade kept reminding herself, "this is just a step, that's all," to keep herself from drifting off the ground like a balloon from the sheer thrill of turning this major page in her life and career.

Once home, she wrote a quick letter to Jere, telling him about Sonny and asked him to come to New York. "Practice up, bro. We might even go on the road together," she wrote.

Jade and Sonny clicked at first. But the more people liked what they heard when Jade performed, the pushier Sonny got. You need to do this, you need to do that. "You need to double on the tenor and soprano sax, maybe flute too so we can get you more gigs with the best groups."

"I don't want to do that," Jade told him. "The alto is my instrument. That's how it is and how I want it to be."

Then he started criticizing her wardrobe, trying to get her to dress up more. "You got great legs, kid. Make that work for you too. You could get yourself a sleek dress at any thrift shop."

"I'm not playing my legs. I've got my Mark VI, remember?" she hoisted her alto mockingly.

"Look, Vi Redd dressed up in sequins and gowns because she knew she had to. Why can't you?"

"Because it's not the 80s anymore. I don't care if it's Trump times and certain men think women have to live and breathe for them. It's my way or none." She was getting pissed, and felt adamant.

Of course Sonny acquiesced—what choice did he have? He did not want to lose his rising star or his gravy train. So Jade wore what she wanted—black or brown tights on top with a vest, jeans, and alternately black or green or red high top sneakers. Whenever Sonny went to see her perform, he closed his eyes because to him, it made her sound that much finer. In his mind, she was a sleek, beautiful young woman dressed to the nines instead of some chick onstage who looked like a misplaced beatnik. He got her gigs and she started to get recognized and popular, although it stung him all the while she was so stubborn she could not see how much more successful she would be if she just listened to him.

Jere came to New York finally, soon after Trump's election. He and Dean found an affordable flat in Brooklyn and moved in with the idea of getting married as soon as possible, before the new administration rescinded their right to do so. Since being with Dean and letting his parents know they were an item, Jere had become politically active. Both had supported Hillary's campaign and were intent on making a statement about their union in a world that was now starting to chip at their human rights and liberties. He told Jade—"Until we get married, I'm putting music aside and concentrating on keeping house."

While Dean brought in most of the couple's money modeling for a top agency, Jere launched a hobby collecting records and music books. At 30, Jere had gained a few inches around his middle and wore a sexy beard stubble. His pale green gray eyes, which now turned slightly downward, were still "show stoppers," as Dean liked to say. His relationship to Dean had calmed and matured him, so now he sometimes called Jade just to check in on her.

"How's my famous sis? Where are you playing next? Can

we come?" Jere's interest delighted Jade. She was thrilled that he seemed to care about her music, her evolution as an artist. He was not, after all, the misogynistic narcissist of his youth who had more patronized than encouraged her. She was always pleasantly surprised to see him, often with Dean, sitting in her audience, watching and listening.

The last night of her run at The Blue Note, she was surprised not see Jere and Dean at the table she knew they had reserved. So, at 11 o'clock, with one more set to go, she checked her cell for messages. There was one from Dean urging her to come to New York Presbyterian Hospital soon as she could.

Jere had been at an anti-Trump demonstration with a bunch of his LGBTQ friends outside the towers bearing the man's name, waving a sign that read, "Rights and equality for all," just as he had at other protests, only this time he had been attacked for it. Upon seeing Jade, Dean said right off the bat, "I guess the wrong people got wind it was a gay team. Jere got beat up pretty bad." He approached Jade, pushing up the sleeves of his blue pullover as if preparing for a big task ahead.

"Oh no," Jade tried to go around him, but he grabbed her by the shoulders. "Wait, let me explain. Trumpers beat the shit out of him."

"But what did he do?" Jade tried to understand.

"The truth is, nothing but protest. He and his friends were just protesting, that's all." Dean let go of her, lowered his head, covering his forehead with one hand. "It's not good," he warned. At the door, she ran into a doctor.

"You are Jade?" An attractive Indian woman shook her hand, gazing at the floor momentarily before looking her square in the eyes. "I'm Doctor Anan. Your brother has several broken bones in his face including a broken nose and he has suffered a severe concussion. He has also lost sight in his right eye. I'm afraid this is going to take some time. Healing will take time," she explained.

"Oh my god. " Jade stepped around the doctor to Jere's bedside. His head was completely bandaged save for his good eye and a space around his nostrils. A nurse on the opposite side of the bed was adjusting his pillows. Only his arms were visible—tubes sticking out of the right; his left arm lay over the cover, palm up. Dean came up behind Jade and gently placed his hand over Jere's.

She had an impulse to hug Jere, but how? He was swathed in bandages and probably in a lot of pain. Still, wanting to connect with him, she went to the foot of the bed and hugged his covered feet.

"Jere, you're going to be okay. We're here. We love you." She heard herself say. Then she began to weep. "Oh my god," she wiped away her tears saying to Dean, "I'm such a baby."

"No, you're not." They spent all night there beside Jere, arranging to take turns the next night and the night after that. Early morning, when Jade finally staggered home, she called Sonny.

"What happened to you?"

"Wow," was all Sonny could say when she relayed about Jere. "Wow," and "wow." Jade didn't care if he was being real or not. She just needed to hear herself tell him what had happened, to ground herself. "It's going to be a long road to recovery and I'm going to have to foot the bills. He doesn't have insurance."

"You're shitting me."

"I'm not. Dean and I are going to have to take care of everything. He was going to get on Dean's insurance, but they had not done it yet. "

There was a long pause on the phone.

"Hello, you there?" Jade said.

"I'm here. I have good news. You're wanted at Blue Whale in LA."

"Wow." It was her turn to be impressed.

"It's a very cool, intimate scene. You would really be spreading your wings." He paused. "Would you consider formal attire?"

Jade sensed he was holding his breath. She thought about Jere, how she needed everything to go smoothly for a while, how an outfit didn't matter in the scheme of things, how she would do anything for her brother.

"Sure, why not."

"That's great!" He could barely contain himself. "You're not going to wear a man's suit or anything like that, are you?" he said.

"No, nothing like that." She laughed at his foolishness and fear. She would wear a dress, something elegant and sharp to highlight her playing.

She let Sonny pick out a black number and heels to match, having warned him she would not go higher than one inch. When she performed in it, she felt only vaguely like a recalcitrant Cinderella. Sonny was right. The applause was mighty, and her CDs sold out after the show. What fools people were about a costume, a façade.

As an artist, she could mold herself into anything. It was like blowing a musical phrase. You blew it, lived in it, and left it for something else. That was what made music beautiful and rare, what made jazz tick too. To stick to a thing too long killed its uniqueness. She understood she had to be fluid, and her feelings about changing her style superficially didn't matter. Music wasn't about ego after all. She would do what she had to do for her brother, that was all.

A year or so after Jere's attack before Trump Towers, Jade, Dean and Jere found themselves lunching together at Prune's on East 1st, commiserating about the not too distant past. Four surgeries later, Jere looked like a slightly tarnished Marlon Brando, tough in a fragile way, the surgeries having smoothed his imperfections so that he was almost too beautiful now. Dean's eyes were ringed with tired circles. He had been working hard. The two were planning an island getaway and were less adamant now about tying the knot in a world that was no longer as supportive about gays as it had been.

"So, how are you," Jade asked her brother. It was the question she always asked first.

"I'm okay, still sad we lost the best woman this country ever had." He picked at his buttered asparagus dish.

"Where's that coming from? That's like history at this point," said Dean.

"It's not old news to me. I was in the hospital post election, and was out of commission for a while," Jere reminded him.

"Yeah, I guess," Dean nodded in assent.

"It's too bad there aren't more women like her. Troopers, you know, that just keep going even when the going gets tough. She's still out there, still fighting, one in a million. If I knew just one other woman like her, I might go straight." He winked at Dean playfully.

"Jere?" Dean addressed him as if he was in a somnolent stupor. "One of those women is sitting right here." He eyeballed Jade at his side.

"Oh please, that's just Jade. She's my sister. She's good at everything. I'm talking about someone who got crushed in a war and is still a champ. I mean, they don't make more than one Hillary, do they?" He plucked up a roll, broke it, and continued with his meal.

Dean rolled his eyes at Jade as if to say, "forgive him, he knows not what he says." But Jade understood. She was there for her brother because she loved him and was a good sister. She herself had thought nothing of it. She was just doing her job. Just as she tried to do the right thing with her music. It didn't matter that Jere was still blind, deaf and dumb to her accomplishments and generosity, or that she had put aside her own desires to go her own way accommodating to Sonny's wishes. These were incidentals and they didn't matter.

None of that mattered. She was long practiced in dealing with ignorance. And she was equally practiced in perseverance. It didn't matter what Jere thought or failed to see, or what Sonny thought either. What mattered was that the music was good, and that Jade did what was right. Nobody had to tell her who she was. After all, she was the one on the stage playing music everybody loved.

She gazed at Jere, his slightly closed right eye that had gained enough vision to see outlines, color, and his other eye that was still vital. No, it didn't matter to her brother that he was half blind. From the outside, you couldn't really tell and that was all that mattered to him.

The Blue Kiss

She stood in a room at The Met glancing at the painting on the wall, which was of two women kissing. From her vantage point, standing slightly away and to the side, the two women lying together interlocked in bed appeared cushioned awkwardly in space, free-floating yet connected.

The painting was by Henri Toulouse-Lautrec, the alcoholic French dwarf artist, and she tried to imagine what it was like living when he did in Paris at the time of the painting, 1892, and what it might have been like for those two prostitutes and others like them who often turned to one another for relief from a world of men.

Mireille, it was reported, was one of the girls in the brothel in the Rue d'Amboise, when Lautrec was commissioned to create a series of panels about the lives of the girls there, and she was one of his favorites. He visited the salons of the brothels in the Rue des Moulins and Rue d'Amboise many times to study and paint the women, who felt very free to be themselves in his company. Many of them, it has been noted, were deeply in love with one another.

Fascinating, it seemed to Helene, that these women who had sex with men, who were paid for their talents as sexual objects, would be so drawn to one another, reveling in same-sex intimacy.

Before and after studying French history in college, Helene had acquired many black and white postcards of the period, images of women scantily clad, boldly unafraid in front of the camera, often indifferent, as if the photographer, or they themselves had been rendered invisible——by what? Their occupation? The camera?

No matter which way Helene eyed the "The Kiss," she could not see the two women save the first way, suspended in space, decontextualized. It seemed odd to her, and compelled by this she came closer to the image. She appreciated Lautrec's art and art in general, as it inspired in her a deeper understanding of music, her métier, and the arts, all things being relational.

As a jazz musician, a tenor sax player, Helene tended toward ballads, having grown up mostly listening to Dexter Gordon. Her father had favored jazz of the bebop and hard bop era, and her mother, who had been an artist before she married, had liked jazz too. Dexter's warm and tender tunes had lullabied her through a turbulent upbringing. In between her parents constant verbal fights about her father's drinking and her mother's infidelities, had been Dexter, telling her everything would be all right.

It wasn't of course. Her mother left when she was nine, and her father died of a brain aneurysm when she was 19. But Dexter opened the way to jazz, and it opened the way to her future even as it sealed away the past.

She wasn't concerned with her own history. What did it matter? Everything had come to a sad end. There was no one beyond her parents. No aunts, uncles, grandparents that she knew of. No traces at all. What a person does then is invent, and music allowed her to do that, make do with the present while asserting herself into the future as it evolved her relationship to jazz.

A person who has nothing can be very optimistic, although it could never be said Helene had nothing. There was the music, and as anybody knows who knows and loves it, music opens up time, and therefore possibilities.

Helene, almost 30 now, was interested in history, the possibilities of these women cast in musical themes in Paris. Their unabashed nakedness moved her. Even when communal, it seemed solitary to her, as if each woman existed alone in her own dimension even while sharing space. That's how the photos in her black and white collection of postcards struck her too.

The women commingled naked in bars leaning close to one another, waiting to be plucked, to go behind curtains with some man. She had observed their profiles, the arc of their hands, the slope of their napes and backs, the roundness of their breasts and buttocks, and thought them beautiful, every one.

Something had been lost between then and now, something in the way women viewed themselves and the world, although not of course in the way the world viewed them. They were still seen as objects rather than processes unfolding in time and space.

Music had taught her that a woman is a body moving through impenetrable space at the speed of light, so fast she diminishes and disappears before you see her. And then she appears, a mystery, to all but herself.

A mere three decades after Toulouse-Lautrec painted the portrait of the two lesbians depicted in "The Kiss," the American Josephine Baker, would be making a jazz sensation in the cabaret bars of Pigalle in Paris, creating a shift in the way women would be viewed, in their role as performers, paving a new path.

But here now, these women in her postcards, these women kissing in the painting, were silent, muted by one another, beautiful in their silence, unable to sing, to articulate beyond their circumstance save as they touched one another.

Helene began to listen to Dexter in her head then performing "I'm A Fool to Want You," as she gazed at the two in the painting. And as she looked on, the image began turning, swirling into a mandala. When it stopped, the painting had opened, and although jazz still played inside her, she was there with the women in their boudoir, an invisible character, listening to their whispered exchanges.

She understood French well enough to capture what they were saying and it amused her that so much of what she was now privy to was speechless, more gestures, the brushing away of hair, a tender caress of the cheek. Such affection.

In her lovemaking with men, Helene had always missed this. The world of men was one of language and then direct sex, void of the erotic. She was erotic. And these women were erotic.

She did not want to disturb them, or be an interloper and began backing out of the room, as if in this way she might return to the present. But immediately, the women gestured waving their arms for her to remain. It was all right. She was welcome.

Absent-mindedly, the one called Mireille with short dark hair, rose, naked, and went to a cupboard beautifully engraved with a large conch and pulled out an unlabeled bottle, Helene took to be wine, and a fine glass that she set on a low, white painted table near Helene, all the while gazing at her lover still waiting on the bed. The other reclined, her spray of autumn hair twisted across a red coverlet, her arms outstretched. On the floor in three or four pale lotus heaps was their thin, tossed apparel. Their eyes locked. Helene's presence sensed by each of them, disturbed nothing.

Helene poured herself a drink and as the women continued their interplay, frolicking, giggling, on the bed, she strolled around the high-ceilinged, ornately-decorated room, which was like a gallery itself with paintings of nudes in various stages of dishabille, here and there with only one breast exposed, in some cases wearing just black stockings or heels. The paintings were elaborately framed too. Lifting a heavy drape before a tall window, Helene could see a snowy street below and a carriage passing by slowly, so slowly it seemed, the driver wearing a top hat struck the two horses in front with a steady beat, as a drummer might strike his snares. A gas lamp directly below illuminated an empty sidewalk.

Indoors, to the side, was a fireplace, its ashes still glimmering. Helene arranged some wood in it, then began to look around for matches. Again, exasperatedly, Mireille jumped up and came over to assist, lighting the fire swiftly, her arms moving expertly. When she was done, she swished her palms together, freeing them of ash. Helene could see a bruise on the back of her left thigh shaped like the heel of a boot, an ungrateful client perhaps, or just the result of play.

The paleness of Mireille's complexion and that of her lover, who was not much older than Helene herself, astonished Helene. It was as if they had always lived indoors. Save for her own hands, her own consciousness, Helene felt little of herself actually in the room, although the women had acknowledged her, made it known they knew she was there.

She wished she had her instrument so she could play for them in this setting, and at that moment her Allora tenor manifested perched on a stand before the fireplace. The fire was crackling now and she felt glad to be a part of this scene, to be able to accompany these women as they made their own kind of music.

Helene removed her beret, which she always wore at gigs, wanting to strip down her persona, let go of her props in these surroundings and stood feet slightly apart, strong legs bent slightly for support in the direction of her audience, and began to play, "Darn That Dream." After that, she would give them, "Don't Explain," then "I'm A Fool To

Want You," the first three cuts on Dexter's album of ballads, which were favorites.

The women had been pecking one another's mouths and cheeks tenderly, but as Helene began to perform for them, they turned toward her eyeing her together and directly for the first time. She could feel the heat of their glance, and made a quick, flicking gesture with her shoulders to remove her vest. The room was getting warmer and she was starting to get into a groove. Mireille and her friend leaned back on the deep, cushioned bed, the tips of their heads touching, their eyes examining something on the ceiling now, as Helene's, Dexter's and Jimmy Van Heusen's music became their muse. One woman's fingers played a trill on the other's bare shoulder. The music had come to them and was now a third lover, weaving them all together.

By the time Helene started to play Billie Holiday's and Arthur Herzog's '"Don't Explain," the women had turned again toward one another and were gazing at one another's eyes and visages thoughtfully, as if in so doing, they might unravel the days and challenges ahead, or perhaps just soften them.

Beads of perspiration formed along Helene's temples as she delivered the music effortlessly, now certain they could not only see her, but hear and feel Dexter's music too that was perfect in its wistful beauty. She was hoping it would feed them, fill them somehow.

At that moment, a rap came at the door, then two, then three in quick succession. Mireille arose and approached the door letting loose a defiant string of, "Non, non, non."

Then her friend got up, and together they moved an armoire against the door to keep it shut. There was a rapid, strong barrage of words between a male and female on the other side, then it dispersed.

Helene kept playing. The women approached holding hands, as if to form a circle around her. Then, impossibly, there appeared as if from nowhere, three, four, a dozen, a score of other women of every color, age, size, variety and description, appending one to the other, hand to hand. As their circle expanded, so did the room, their arms and filaments of their hair spinning out into the night, turning into the vast milky way of the universe. And all the while jazz played, the fire sang, and outdoors, snow fell silently and the hooves of horses stamped notes on the staff of the white streets of Paris.

Foolish Love

That winter we lived among mice in the Berkshires, in a little cabin set not far from a large white clapboard house that belonged to the owner, Betty, who was a widow. Two steps up to the cabin did nothing to keep the mice away. Their constant tweaking and bustle made me feel I was living in an indoor forest. Betty, who was a nice old lady, warned us. "You'll never be able to keep the mice out. If you can stand them, the place is yours."

We had come up to the Berkshires figuring we might have to rough it, but had no idea. Van and I had been together about two years then. The summer before we had been married on a beach in Provincetown by a drunken preacher who moonlighted as a cabaret singer. Two months after that, I miscarried. By the end of summer, we'd run up all the tabs we could in Brewster, where we lived in my apartment. The landlord had given me an ultimatum, but without jobs we couldn't pay rent. So we split.

Seniority and the fact our one vehicle belonged to Van meant he made all the major decisions. It was his idea to get off the Cape to turn a page, maybe even get jobs offseason. I didn't care much where we went as long as long as we were together. I'd spent my whole life babysitting and working my ass off, raising three younger brothers and a sister after our mom died of the big C. Our dad, a drunken sloth, had run away long before that. By the time I met Van, the twins were 17, living on their own, the older one, Chad, getting ready to join the navy. I'd been waitressing since I was 15. Van was my hard-earned vacation, although no one I knew at the time ever failed to point out what a fool I was leaving my job at The Sand Bar just because Van said so, so I could be there at his beck and call. Foolish love.

Van was an only child, raised among chickens, goats and pines on a New Hampshire farm. His parents were in their 40s when they had him, so he was spoiled. As an adult, he always came home. After college, he hitchhiked around Europe for a while, then came back to live with his parents, helping out a little, gardening and feeding animals, nothing that ever got to be routine. He didn't strike out again until he was 30. He was 44 when I met him, 20 years my senior, and still getting an allowance from his folks.

I thanked my lucky stars when I met Van. The universe had finally delivered on my prayers for something better, someone who would appreciate me. My mother had died a few months before and I was feeling tired and old. First time I saw him he was sitting in a director's chair at an outdoor art show in Wellfleet, wearing shades and drinking from a can of Coors in a paper bag. I knew it was Coors because the can was tall and in those days that was the only tall brand.

His seascapes were a little dull, but technically pretty good. Art had been my major at Cape Cod Community, so I wasn't intimidated by him. One painting had a red barn in a field and I liked that one, probably because there was a human in it, a boy holding a stick. Later, I learned he'd done all the work years before when he was an art student. He just needed the money.

"Is that you?" I asked pointing at the dark haired kid in the barn painting, just to make conversation.

"Maybe," he said and took a swig. Then we got to jawing.

He wasn't like the older men I knew who grabbed me wherever whenever I passed by with a tray of drinks. Van was cool, longish hair, sun streaked. My roommate Shelly called him "sinister," but I never paid attention to her or anybody's opinion of him. I'd been telling myself I should be with somebody mature, who wasn't a part of the bar scene. Of course Van drank more than all the guys I'd ever known put together, but there was no way for me to know that in the beginning. Coors and a Marlboro the minute his legs swung over the edge of the bed getting up, every day. Usually, we drank "rot gut" bourbon or whiskey, which Van liked. Whenever Van and I got together, booze was always there like an extra charge. I'd always loved drinking, but before Van it was mostly social, ales and shots of whatever friends did late nights at bars.

Even weekdays, Van couldn't stay away, ringing my doorbell in the wee hours when it was still dark, even though my first shift started at seven. I'd open the door wearing nothing but a faded red and blue Sox t-shirt, rubbing my eyes, "what are you doing here?"

He'd lean against the door jamb, wreaking of booze, cigarettes and his salty male scent that I liked, his eyes slits from alcohol and desire. "Nothing baby. I just wanted to see the sun rise and there you are." He'd take me in his arms and we'd make beautiful, tender love. Then I'd make him coffee.

He had a strong, broad chest and when I rested my head on it sometimes I placed my hand on the lower part of his sternum. My index and middle finger fit perfectly into the small dent in the middle, which I initially took to mean God wanted me to be there for him to protect his vulnerability, to complete him. That's how I really thought in those days when my love of him increased my faith in everything and made me ridiculous to myself even. Van liked falling asleep, my long hair twined in his hand like a stirrup so I couldn't go anywhere. I should have known then we were headed for trouble.

Even though I let Van make all the major decisions, I spoke up when Betty warned us about the mice. "Maybe this is a sign," I said. "I'm not spending winter killing anything but time." He knew I couldn't tolerate seeing a dead thing. I wasn't a Buddhist then, so it wasn't quite about the killing yet. Van knew if we stayed, he would have to do something about the vermin. "Sheila, honey, I promise, you will never see a dead thing." Well, he was almost right.

What I did see and hear each day and night was the sound of traps slapping shut and the sandwich bags in which they'd been placed racing around like strange entities over the crappy rug of the main room—surreal. One step up was a small, windowless kitchen and to its right, a compact bathroom. One step up from that was a square bedroom with a queen-sized bed, one small narrow dresser, and a two by two-foot TV, which sat at the foot of the bed before an orangey curtain behind which was a closet barely deep enough to hide a person. I don't know what we thought we would do in that place except drink, which was probably the point, although we did try having a life at first.

We found jobs together right away, Van as a chef and me waitressing at a big campground nearby. Van could flip eggs and flapjacks in a pan and look expert, but he wasn't much of a cook. The restaurant was big but the rushes were with polite customers, so I thought we had a pretty good gig. Then, second or third week in, manager caught Van filching a bottle of Jack Daniels and we both got the boot. Words spreads like fire in the biz, so we thought we'd try drinking fulltime after that, stuck in a cabin where the heat never went above 60-degrees in the coldest winter I remember in my lifetime.

One time I found on old pair of snowshoes in the closet Betty said we could keep. "Come on, let's check out the woods. You wear one and I'll wear the other," said dumb ass. He broke his trying to force it on his big foot, stomping on it, and anyway while my snowshoe and Van's snowshoe that he'd strapped on with packing tape stayed on the surface, our other boots sunk two feet into the snow. So we really couldn't go far into the woods and besides were coughing our brains out from all our smoking and just that minor exertion. "Maybe we'll spot some squirrels or rabbits or even a bear," said Van. Wishful thinking.

One night, I went to take a pee, switched on the bathroom light and almost had a heart attack. There was a mouse dead on its side in the toilet bowl, one open eye staring up at me. I made Van wrap him in a rag and toss him in the outdoor bin. "No doubt that mouse committed suicide from the cold," I said. In my mind's eye, it was big enough to have been a rat.

On the Cape, with my brothers and sister, and when they grew up and left, cousins, bar friends and their dramas to keep me going season to season, hot or cold, good or bad, I'd never thought much about winter. Here, Van and I only had each other. We drank more and fought more. Had it not been for the space of eternity between houses on Pleasant Street, the ironic name of the street where we lived, Betty and the rest of our neighbors would have had a good earful of our business. Maybe they did and I just don't know it.

We got to drinking and fighting earlier and earlier in the day. We fought about old issues—no money, no work and how paranoid I had become, so paranoid I couldn't leave the house and even had Van watch me take a pee whenever I could get him to because I was afraid I'd die if I was left alone. He would just look down at me shaking his head, like I was the most pathetic thing he'd ever seen. I was in a constant state of nerves from drinking, and since losing the baby, was convinced that if left alone, I would perish. It didn't even make sense, but that didn't matter to my feelings.

Maybe I wanted to die. There's a saying in AA, "sick and tired of being sick and tired." I was so messed up, and wanted Van, who was older and who should have known better, to make things right——which was like wishing for the impossible because the only thing Van cared about was Van. He was the first real narcissist I ever knew—good-looking, sexy, but selfish to the core. Once in a while his parents sent a small check, which he used for booze for himself. We were always scraping for groceries as all our money went to booze and cigs. Betty let me clean her three bathrooms once a week and Van shoveled snow from the paths leading to and from the cabin and her house, so we basically traded for rent.

Halfway through a half gallon of Tavola Red wine, or a pint of bourbon, Van would start. "Why can't you get a job? I pay for everything. I got the wheels, I got the bucks. What do you have? I should pimp your ass. What else are you good for?"

"You're the worse kind of white trash, pretending to be white trash when you're nothing but a spoiled brat," I told him. I laughed in his face, reminded him his money was his parents, his car was his parents and all he had was me and he should be grateful. Then I stopped bothering. Fighting with him wasn't worth it. I let myself sink into the one comfortable chair in the main room, hid behind cigarette smoke, a drink or a book, sometimes all three. I just couldn't wait for him to pass out. Once in a while, I niggled him. "Then why did you ever chase me in the first place?" He never had an answer for that, would just turn away, like he hadn't heard.

One night Van really struck low. "You worthless piece of shit, you can't even be a mother."

To which I responded by hurling the closest thing to me I could find, which turned out to be a Tavola Red bottle. I couldn't even think straight. It was like I was defending my dead boy, Robbie, what I would have named our child. We drove to the hospital, or rather he did, with me at his side in his hand-me down Buick, mopping up blood from his head with one of his old shirts, trying to keep it off the seats. I told him I was sorry, although I wasn't sure what for.

Van's mouth cost him six stitches. We didn't talk to each other for about a week after that. What was there to miss? All he did was play his records of Charlie Parker, Ornette Coleman and this new cat, Keith Jarrett, who was very inventive on the piano. Van loved jazz, and I dug it too, even though none of those cats touched my soul. Only Billie did. Van never played Billie, but I came upon her *Lady Sings the Blues* album in his stash one night when there was nothing I could do to fall asleep and he was out cold.

My one comfort was being alone at night, with pitch blackness blanketing the cabin. I preferred blackness any day to the sight of cold white space stretching to infinity. Darkness and night were familiar. With Van out of it, there was nothing but the crackling universe at hand. I felt freer and calmer then.

Billie confirmed for me what a terrible world it was. Her song, "Strange Fruit," cut through me. There was someone whose race had suffered far more than anyone in mine ever could. There was real suffering and trouble in her voice. But the songs that really drew me to her were "God Bless the Child" and "Good Morning Heartache." Listening to them made me feel Billie and I were sisters, shared the same sorrows, and I did not feel alone. After I was done listening to Billie, done crying my eyes out over her beautiful voice and the awful state of the world, I would put the record back in its jacket and tuck it away back on the shelf. I didn't want Van to know I had listened to it or even liked it. Billie was my secret.

It's a good thing alcoholics forget so much that happens to them. I was in the worst shape of my life with Van in that cabin, where the only body heat I got was curling up next to him when we slept or he or I passed out or the rare times he was drunk and wanted to get it on, which was less and less because with each passing day he drank more, got drunk quicker and passed out sooner. He was stages ahead of me as a drunk, even though I couldn't take it nearly as well physically. I spent half the time wanting to die from the pain of hangovers. There was so much alcohol in my system, I'd step out of a shower and 10 minutes later my waist-length hair would be dry, my alcohol-laden pores having absorbed all the moisture. I didn't have to use a hairdryer until months after I got sober.

Van never seemed to suffer hangovers like me probably because he was always drunk. Even so, he found things to do with his hands, made himself at least a little useful, and wasn't afraid like me of stepping out into the world. I had gone from being one of the most productive people I knew to being utterly useless. Really the only thing that soothed me was Billie. I wondered if Billie had ever seen such white-ness as this, like death, the end of everything, and thought what a fool I was to even consider she had not.

One night, Van started pelting me with questions—"Why are we here? Why are you with me? Why? Answer me." I couldn't. I didn't even know what he was getting at. His wide eyes and tense body leaning toward me frightened me. Signs were all there he was about to blow a gasket, so I ran into the bedroom, which had no door to close. He followed of course, pushed me back on the bed, leaning over, his hands fists, mouth, a slash of rage, "Why? Why are we here? Why are you with me?"

"I don't know. I don't know. I haven't done anything," I kept trying to calm him. He growled, a deep, troubled, unforgiving sound. Turning as if to find some support for his anger, he snatched the heavy orangey curtain of our one bedroom window off its hooks, threw it over me and himself on top of it.

"Van, I can't breathe." I really couldn't. I was sure he was out of his mind and didn't know what he was doing. Wriggling, I managed to slip out from under him, off the bed, and back to the main room while he continued raging, arms splayed bearing down on the curtain as if it didn't mat-ter who was under it or even that there was nobody. It was just alcoholic madness needing to express itself. He was in a black out.

When he was functional, Van tinkered, repairing appli-ances, or lamps he'd broken during a fight the night before. He liked to sit with his penknife, carving things, boats, cars and crosses that sat unfinished on the windowsill. It was more than I could do—I, who at one point been able to hold down a job while raising four siblings as if they were my own. Where had that self gone?

I kept busy doing little insignificant things, making salads, soups, trying to read. Mostly, I stared aghast at the white world through the back picture window wondering what had become of us, of me. I remember once holding a paperback of Isak Dinesen's *Winter's Tales* open on my lap on the same page for a good hour unable to get beyond the first paragraph, my brain was so scrambled.

"I'm losing my mind, Van," I said.

"And that's news?"

We were so bored with one another, with drinking even, and our cold, static reality, which we could not escape. Everything indoors was brown, ossified, as we were. Brown mice. Brown bags enshrouding them. Old brown mangy rug. Brown table and chairs. Brown walls, shelves, books, and desk. Brown lamps, even their shades. Everything cheap, basic, plain, save the desk, which was not only functional but large, with deep drawers that sat empty. We dragged around heavy brown army blankets like old soldiers perambulating in a strange and foreign war. Our minds were brown too, soggy from drink, indulgence, stupefied by sameness, dullness, sadness. Somewhere beneath the brown architecture, hidden in the hollows of anger and horror, coursed sadness like a latent spring. Nothing was alive here but our voices and white cold out there, screaming.

And Billie's voice? A dream of something possible, not

quite here, a trace of the past, one soul's anguish pointing to the future. Find a way to sing, it said. That's the only way out of this prison.

Sensing or hearing our misery, and knowing we couldn't afford to go out, Betty made the neighborly effort once a week to bring us homemade soup. One day she called to say she couldn't bring soup over because she was sick. I told her not to worry and made pea soup for her instead, happy to be able to do her a favor. All it took were a few carrots, a chopped potato and some onion slivers. Pea soup was cheap and I made it often.

I felt reckless carrying over the pot with my brew over to Betty's, walking that far from the cabin on my own. It felt like a bold move.

"Come in, child. Gracious, you're blue. Look what you did. Oh, just look." Betty clapped her little, immaculately-manicured hands together with glee. In my excitement to show her what I had made, I raised the lid of the pot, but couldn't manage a solid or steady grip with just one hand around the handle, I shook so badly. The whole thing crashed, spilling all over Betty's beautiful, polished hardwood foyer floor. It could have been the pearl white shag rug of her living room, in which case she would surely not have forgiven me.

I spent the next half hour on my hands and knees with a roll of paper towels wiping up green slop while biting my upper lip to fight back tears while Betty kept repeating, "it's all right, it's the thought that matters," in her sweet way. I knew soon as I left, she would get down on her hands and knees,

165

sick and all, and get that floor really spanking clean. She must have known how miserable I felt because when I finally got up from the floor, she led me by the hand to a little bar in the next room and offered me some peach schnapps.

"Take this thimbleful. It'll get you back in shape." That's what she called a shot and I took it, gladly. The bottle was a little less than half full and she offered it to me. "You and Van need it more than I do. To keep warm," she added, as if explanation was necessary.

I kept the schnapps at the foot of the bed in one of my rubber boots. By then we were both hoarding booze, keeping it from one another. Whenever Van went to the liquor store, he always came back drunk. He kept a pint for himself under the car seat too.

One day I sat at the desk looking out the back window at white woods. Sometimes I sat there with a notebook and pen staring at the too bright page of the world wondering if I might ever be able to write a coherent thought or idea. All I could see was winter. I was crying silently, not wanting to let Van know I was crying because it would upset him. Anyway, while I sat there, miserable in my well of self-pity, a deer tiptoed out of the woods and sat or knelt by the cabin looking at me with the warmest, kindest eyes. We looked at one another for a while, then I went and got a couple of carrots from the only bag of anything I could find in the fridge and tossed them in the deer's direction to thank him for his kindness. The next day the deer was still there, so I threw him the rest of the carrots. Van got pissed, saying why was I wasting our food on a sick deer, but I didn't care.

The third day another deer was sitting with the first and there were four sets of eyes gazing at me pitifully asking me what I was going to do with the rest of my life. I took a good look at Van passed out at 10 in the morning, spilling out from the chair on which I normally sat reading. Empty Lite beer cans covered the shitty rug where more mice had died than soldiers in the Civil War. I made up my mind then, went to the phone book and called the first shrink my finger came upon and when Van woke up told him I had an appointment to get a prescription for Valium for us, knowing that would be the only way I'd get him to take me to see a doctor.

Dr. Paul—I don't remember his last name—was a nice Jewish shrink who saw the situation right away and told me straight up if I didn't stop drinking or get away from Van, I would probably die. "At the rate you're going, you won't see 30. You can't be 100 pounds soaking wet," he said. I hadn't realized I'd been feeding Van most of what we ate and losing weight. I would probably have done anything to get away from the hellhole we had created, but I couldn't do it alone. As they say in AA, I was ready to surrender.

Dr. Paul and I devised a plan, and one afternoon the following week he picked me up when Van was out shopping. I had started to stop drinking, taking only a couple of glasses of wine and Valium to get me to sleep at night and help me deal with withdrawal. It took less than five minutes to get everything I owned into a small knapsack, plus the Billie Holiday album, which I stole because it was the only thing Van owned that I felt really belonged to me.

I was so grateful to Dr. Paul for getting me into a halfway house, although the second day a bad case of DT's, hallucinations and tremors sent me to the hospital for a while. Then it was back to rehab. I knew Van wouldn't chase after me once I was gone. I mean, why would he have bothered? Just leaving him felt like I'd emerged from a long black tunnel into light. Everything behind me turned to ashes. I began waitressing again, little by little regaining my self respect and self esteem.

Looking back on that time, the feelings are all there, although my memory of Van's voice, his form, his tenderness, were all but obliterated by what happened during our season of discontent crushing love like a sledgehammer. He's gone. But I remember Billie, her songs like flocks of geese disappearing into the empty sky, wings flapping in unison, warning of revolution. I remember her and the deer.

Bitches' Brew

Allie drove her taxi with a smart ass attitude, smacking gum ceaselessly, and wore a Yankees cap backwards on her head on the job, even though she'd never watched baseball in her life, didn't even like the game. Her dad had named her after a pitcher who'd won five straight World Series and Allie was always grateful she hadn't been named Lefty or something like that.

Allie's father had been the true baseball fan and Allie wore his cap in his memory. His real gift to her was love of music, jazz in particular. In her cab, she listened to WBGO, 88.3, remembering times she hung out with her dad in their garage listening to Miles Davis, Chick Corea, Wayne Shorter, experiments in sound, beautiful chaos while he fixed things. The garage was Bert's space and his peace, or rather, the music was, and the smoke and silence that rose between them accentuated this. Whenever the strangers she drove around asked about her father, Allie always said, "He went the way of the Marlboro man." Cancer.

It surprised people to learn that she, a Millennial should enjoy jazz. "Jazz was like my Gerber food," she liked to say. As a teen she dug hip hop enough to explore its fusion with jazz, but the fusion didn't make sense to her—each genre took from rather than contributed to the other. It was like oil and water, like her ma and pop.

She understood as she got older that it was in fact she who held them together because her parents really had nothing in common. He was a man obsessed with music, with what could have been, and he tried to fix everything as if it in doing so he could re-create his past. He had wanted to be a musician himself, and played bass once, before opting for the straight life. A family was a sure legacy, his father had told him. Music was not.

Bert's wife, Lenore, loved only her offspring and traditions from which she felt removed, a fact that sometimes made her bitter. When Allie's father passed away, Lenore felt abandoned, but she was also free to be herself, a simple woman whose appreciations were limited to whatever was right in front of her and to whatever felt familiar.

Allie's father passed away when Allie was a junior at NYU, and after that, she dropped out and started driving cabs for a living. It mattered neither to her nor to her mother that she would probably never finish college. What did she need that for? She had already come to terms with life as it served itself daily to her on a slightly tarnished platter. She understood that life gave and took away mercilessly and without bias and that it would be wise to always remember this. Even at her still young age, she never wavered from just feeling lucky to be alive. She drove a cab and came home to meals with her mother and dug the routine of her days because for the while she couldn't fathom any other, even if sometimes with no one else to nag, her mother got on her case.

"Take off that filthy cap. Have some respect, Allie. Give it to me, let me wash it for you." But like a child with its blanket, Allie refused to have her mother appropriate the thing that meant something to her beyond the fact of what it was. Soon enough, her mother flipped to maternal inquiries ——"You OK, all right? Nobody tried to blow your head off today? No customers tried to rob you?" To which Allie typically responded, "I'm OK, ma. How are you?" looking her straight in the eye, like her father used to do. "Is there anything I can get you, ma?" thinking to herself——a joint? Some whiskey? A man?

"I don't need nothing until God in heaven wills it," was her stock reply. In her mind, if Allie lost her job, God would feed them, God would pay the rent, God would take care of their business——not the government, not anyone else. In Allie's mother's mind, the money Allie made was extra to what she already had in her God bank because to her blessings were everything.

When weather was bad, Allie heard, "You drive safe. This city is crazy. Half the people shouldn't even be on the road." Since the elections, they kept up political banter——"Did you hear what that idiot in the White House said today? I should have never left Cuba."

The truth was Allie's mother's moods never rubbed Allie the wrong way. Her carryings on were predictable, a counterpoint to the voices that made nightly rounds in Allie's head and sometimes made it hard for her to sleep. Her daily repertoire at work played like music. One long weekend when her mother took off to visit her sick aunt on Long Island, Allie took a stay-at-home break and it was like she was at a jazz club. Conversations she'd had with passengers ran in her head, sometimes jointly like two discs spun by a DJ, sometimes in double time, establishing themselves in her memory like hit songs she could replay, amplifying when she was alone:

"No," she shook her head, emphatically. "Nothing else but *Bitches Brew* far as fusion is concerned. I love that album."

"You see, you see," the hip hop guy said jumping up and down on the seat behind her, while poking up his shades at the ridge so they'd stay fixed and cool. "That's fusion, man."

"No, man, it's New York. That's why it works. It's like the city, aggressive and unpredictable. And like this job, man."

The breathless duo who took that rider's place informed her, "Dig it, that was Jay Z, the man himself. Did you know that?"

She eyed them in the rear view, a bi-racial couple, she, African-American, a leggy beauty dressed to the nines, and he, in a tux with a bow tie cinching his throat so it looked he might choke at any moment. His face was deeply flushed. The scent of her dusky perfume and hard booze commingled in the cab.

"Jay Z. Wow. The seat's still warm, baby."

"I know it," she said, squirming, letting her rabbit fur slip a little from one shoulder as she adjusted herself, feeling out the moment.

"Wow," he repeated. "He and Beyonce must have had a fight. I mean why else would he take a cab?" He tapped the shield between them. "No offense," he said to Allie.

"None taken," she replied.

Then she had a passenger named Yolanda whose laughter she could not forget. Allie picked her up on West 10th as she attempted to disentangle herself from what looked like a mélange of relatives. She was one of those people who immediately latch onto something personal and use it as a key to launch into the warm and intimate. Her gentle rolling laughter was like orange jello shaking in a generous bowl, and she had a broad, kind face to boot. She sat in back embracing her large pocket book, keeping it like a little family close to her bosom the whole way back to Brooklyn.

"Anybody ever tell you, you look like Carrie Fisher, the star?"

"The writer slash comedian slash actress who died? Naw." Allie let a beat pass. "I'm just joshing with you. I hear that all the time, like every day."

"Her death was such a tragedy, tsk tsk. And her mother aftah her." More tsking.

"My mother just about had a heart attack."

"My mother too, honey. You live with your mama?"

"I do."

"That's a good girl. Children and parents should always live together."

"Do your children live with you?"

"Oh no. I have five boys. They are all on their own. A couple are married, thank the good Lord. With males, it's different, you know. If you take care of them, they never marry. They has to find a woman of their own."

"Is that right? I wouldn't know."

"You an only child, honey?"

"I am, and a grateful one."

"You didn't miss no games and laughter growing up?"

"My mama played all the games and I did all the laughing, no problem there."

Hahahaha. "And do you and your mamita get along."

"Well enough, I guess."

"A mother/daughter relationship is so special. I wish I had girls of my own."

"No doubt. Five boys is a handful."

"You telling me. I got one who's a barber, married, in Jersey. Tommy in Georgia, married just last year. One in the navy. The second to last, Jimmy, is an accountant. And the youngest, Andrew, is an actor and gay."

"Oh yeah?"

"Yeah. That was never a problem for me. But his father…."

"That is sometimes a problem in Latino families."

"You know, you are so wise for your age and you look so very young."

"Thank you."

"And you know, it shouldn't be a problem in these cultures where family is so strong. They should be more forgiving, more accepting."

"I agree."

"Well, all I have to say is your mother must be very proud to have such a smart girl. What is your name, dear? I will keep you in my prayers."

She told her.

"And mine is Yolanda. God bless you and your family."

"And you and yours too."

"And here is an extra something for your niceness."

"Thank you, Yolanda."

Allie liked the Yolandas who reveled in the joys of maternity and all things good in the universe. She could always count on being delighted by them, no matter what was happening in the moment.

Allie could forget a face but never a voice, so she was pleasantly surprised when a couple of weeks after her vacation at home, she heard Yolanda's mellifluous voice greeting her in the back of the cab. She could see in her rear view that it was indeed the nice lady from Brooklyn, although at first she did not recognize her because she was weeping.

The crying was like no other Allie had heard before, full throated and bellied, her whole being thrown into it.

"Are you OK, ma'am?" Allie inquired politely.

"I'll be OK. I'll be OK. A mother has a right to cry, doesn't she?"

"Yes, absolutely."

Yolanda wiped her eyes with the hook of her index finger, then blew her nose. "Thank you for understanding. You are so understanding. Oh," she shook a finger Allie's way, "You're that young girl from before, Alexandra."

"Allie."

"That's right. Oh, I'm sorry, hon, to make a scene. It's my boy, Andrew the gay one. He disappeared."

"Oh no."

"Oh yes. For days. I went crazy. His brothers went crazy. His father was going to go to the police. What do you think happened?"

"I don't know. He eloped?"

"Oh my god. How did you know? That's exactly what happened. He eloped. But not with a girl. With a man. So you can imagine."

"I can. I guess your husband and sons are having a hard time."

"Hard time? They are getting ready to disown him. My baby. Why didn't he tell me? Why couldn't he confide in his mother?" Again tears in cascades that Allie imagined overrunning the back of the cab.

"I'm so sorry. It's pretty common nowadays for gays to marry, so your family should just get used to that."

"That's what I said. But you know how men can be. My husband is also from Cuba. There are rules. Certain things he can not imagine, does not want to imagine."

"Which is probably why your son took off to do this on his own, right? I would have done that too."

Yolanda leaned forward, grabbing the back of Allie's seat, intrigued. "Do you mind if I ask you something, honey?"

"Shoot."

"Are you a homosexual?"

"Um. I really don't know how to answer that because I

haven't given it a lot of thought. But yeah, most of the people I've slept with have happened to be ladies. I did have sex with a cop once, a guy, who turned out to be gay."

"Oh my goodness, dear. I hope you used protection."

"Of course. He wasn't gay then. We grew up together. He came out a little after that."

"I see. And you didn't see him as marriage material."

"No, no way."

"So is marriage something you yourself would not consider?"

"Oh sure. Yeah. Right girl, woman, whatever. Sure."

"So you would like marry someone of your own gender and whatchamacallit, proclivity, is that right?"

"Right."

"Listen, honey, can I ask youse a favor. It's a big one."

Allie hesitated but was curious. "OK."

"I need to talk to the men in my house. I don't want to lose my son. It sounds as if you have had some experience. Would you consider backing me up."

"Whoa, no. I'm so sorry, ma'am. That is not something I could do. No way."

"I see." She sat back, placid, deflated. "I thought you understood. Thank you for your wisdom. I apologize for the intrusion."

Allie could hear her pulling Kleenex after Kleenex out of her purse, crying silently in the back of the cab. The ride would last another five minutes or so, but Allie was not sure she could tolerate it. Nothing worse than a woman crying, especially a nice one, especially when you are contributing to the tears.

"Listen, Mrs.—"

"Yolanda."

"Yolanda. I'm sorry to hurt your feelings. But I'm just a cab driver. I don't know shit. Really."

Yolanda waved her hand apologetically before her face. "I'm sorry. I thought you were very wise. My mistake. I thought you had empathy."

"I do have empathy. I totally understand why your son did what he did. Families can be difficult."

"Please, I do not wish to be rude. But I cannot bear to hear you speak, knowing you have answers that could possibly save my family that you are not willing to share——" Then she added quietly, in a voice tinged with pain and regret, "with others, with them."

Allie blinked looking through the windshield. She was approaching West 10th again, where she would let Yolanda off to commiserate with her relatives. Clouds were in the distance. Rain. She blinked into the rearview where she could see a portrait of resignation, darkly alone, fixing on her.

Allie cleared her throat and then, unbelievably, heard herself pursue the matter. "What exactly would you expect me to do?"

Yolanda eyed her warily, her large expressive eyes shifting momentarily to scan the outdoors before returning to her driver.

"I would like to take you to brunch this Sunday. We meet at Victor's once a month because my husband has a cousin who is the chef there."

"I work until five p.m. every other Sunday. This Sunday is OK."

"Wonderful. We meet at one. I'll introduce you as a friend. Simple."

"Please do not put me on the spot, or I will walk out. I'm not a mediator. I can't promise anything but that I'll be there."

"You are a blessing. Trust me. You have no idea. I will see you at 1 PM for brunch at Victor's. This Sunday. Thank you so much. Hasta pronto, my dear."

The entire way over to Victor's Allie kept repeating to herself, "It's a free meal, free meal, free meal," like a mantra. She was dressed in what was typical formal attire for her—trousers, a white shirt, gold tie. At the last minute, she decided to drop the tie. It would do no good to antagonize the males in Yolanda's family from the outset. She gazed at herself in the front window of Victor's, ran a hand through her short punkish hair, took a deep breath and entered.

Almost right away, a male host took her hand, smiled a very white smile and led her to a large table, where sat Yolanda, a portly man with a broad face wearing a constricted expression—Yolanda's husband, she gathered—and a nervous young man with nicotine-stained fingers and vaguely handsome features behind dark-rimmed glasses—her son, Jimmy.

"Our son Ron, who is in the navy, and of course the two married boys will not be coming." After a pause she added, "We are waiting for Andrew," which made Andrew sound like the Pope.

"We are not waiting to order," announced her husband, and it was clear from his tone that they would not.

Yolanda tapped one of Allie's hands reassuringly. "Whatever you like, my dear. We start with appetizers. This is an excellent menu."

Allie started off with corn grits and shrimp in enchilada sauce. The others all had fried plantain topped with bits of pork. The conversation was jovial and general——the weather of the day, which was idyllic; the political tenor——thankfully they were on the same page, so each one tossed an adjective to add to the consensus of "disaster." There were polite inquiries about jobs. They toasted and drank Margaritas and were on a second round waiting for entrées of Cuban quesadillas, when a frenetic young man with a cherubic face and dyed blond hair joined the group. Andrew.

He went straight over to his mother, kissing her twice on each cheek, then approached the father who stretched out a hand to indicate distance, so Andrew merely tapped his shoulder. His brother Jimmy nodded at him cordially. There was no embrace there either. Andrew sat next to Allie.

"I've heard a lot about you," he said to her with a conspiratorial air. "So glad to have a friend join the family." He smiled. A very nice guy, clearly, expressive like his mother.

"What are you drinking," said Yolanda. "And eating, honey. You look thin."

"I'm not, ma. I'll have the same thing everybody else is having. Skip the appetizer."

Yolanda ordered for him. Then there was a dense pause. Allie continued eating, her antenna out as if she was driving, looking out for potential accidents on the road.

"Ma says you drive a cab. Very cool."

"It pays the rent. And it's fun."

"It's nice to do what you like. The one bringing in real bucks in this family is that one," Andrew pointed to his brother. Jimmy acknowledged him with a slight fake smile.

"Of course, dad is retired," Andrew added as an afterthought.

"Hey congrats," said Allie said a little to the side, referring to his marriage.

"Thank you," he bowed slightly in her direction, putting the napkin on his lap as his drink arrived. He sipped it eagerly, then said, "cheers everybody, and to our new friend, Allie."

They were all eating their main meal now, and presently, they brought Andrew his plate.

"Frankly, if you were hoping she gets together with Jimmy, she's getting along better with that one. You should tell her, it's hopeless," said Roland to Yolanda out of the corner of his mouth, but loud enough for everyone to hear.

"It is what it is," said Yolanda to the space in front of her.

Had this been a set up to help, or a set up for a date, Allie began to wonder.

They were all digging the quesadillas, which were out of this world, eating like it was the most important task at hand. In the midst of the symphony of mastication, Yolanda began.

"It so happens Allie has much in common with Andrew. They are, if I can put it this way, one of a kind." She put a napkin to her mouth briefly and then coughed a little before adding, "Very special people are hard to find."

Allie smiled nervously. She thought she felt Andrew's foot tap hers under the table.

Yolanda went on with grace and precision, "There are at least three of us at this table who believe a good marriage can exist with any two people who love each other. Is that right?"

Allie nodded slightly.

"Ma," said Jimmy. It was a warning.

"Oh gosh, is this what we're going to talk about—while eating, no less," said Roland.

"Apparently," said Andrew.

Immediately, Yolanda made fists of her hands at either side of her plate, her eyes brightening with a rim of tears. "I have five sons and unless, heaven forbid, I lose one to death before I myself pass, they will always be my sons until the day I kick! There is no way you can deny a mother, her son," she said to everyone and no one in particular.

Roland was shaking his head, pushing his plate a little away. He pointed a quivering hand at Andrew.

"Look what you've done. See how unhappy your mother is."

"He has done nothing to make me unhappy. I'm unhappy about you, and you," she turned to her husband, then Jimmy, whose color was draining fast.

"The kind of support I need is not from him. Andrew has always supported his mother."

Andrew smiled broadly at everyone.

"You and you are a disgrace. Gay marriage is an everyday thing now."

"Shhh." Both her husband and Jimmy tried to shush her at her mention of the word that was like foul language.

"It is. I'll say it again if I want. You are backwards people. I do not want you in my house if you cannot accept my son. And this is what I have to say to you today. To you, Roland. my husband of almost 30 years. And to you my supposedly smart other son."

Their mouths dropped. Neither Roland nor Jimmy knew what to say at first.

"Ma, what are you saying?" Jimmy spoke up.

Roland waved her away. "Don't be ridiculous. I pay the bills. You can't live in that house alone. I'm not going anywhere and that's that."

"Then I will go. Unless you accept my son Andrew and his decision, and his partner, Jose, I will leave our house."

"Apologies," Roland said offhandedly to Allie. "This is family business. As often happens, family business can get out of hand."

"You are welcome," Yolanda told Allie. She turned to her husband, "She is my guest."

"Yes," chimed Andrew.

"And where may I ask would you go, Miss Independence."

"I will go live with my friend." She pointed to Allie.

Now it was Allie's turn to respond and she put a napkin delicately to her mouth and said, "yes," simply, like this had all been pre-arranged.

"You would leave me to go live with a, a——"

"A young woman who loves her mother and respects gays. Yes."

"Ma," said Jimmy. "Think this through. You're talking crazy."

"Is anybody listening to me," said Yolanda.

"Yes," said Allie again.

"Yes," said Andrew.

In the middle of this cacophony of voices, Allie began to hear what sounded like horns honking, a mad line of taxis squeezing one another, and somebody snapping fingers signaling a stop or start. And a train passing, drums. She was smack in the center of the city she loved, doing what she knew best, listening to what she loved best, Miles's "Bitches Brew" coming surely from the distance of the speakers. And she thought, "wow," how the music was here now, to give the moment some heresy, sense, and truth, providing unification, fusion. And how it was up to her again, she who was always in the middle, and who in spite of herself led the way, like the master himself.

Roland ran his hands exasperatedly through his gray crew cut. "Yes, I'm listening and I don't like what I hear. But I respect you. You are my wife."

"And this is your son. Who also deserves respect." She acknowledged Andrew, then reminded Jimmy—"This is your brother."

Then Yolanda said to her husband, "At least be man enough to shake hands. Be decent enough to make a start. Nobody is getting kicked out of this family. As long as I'm alive, this family stays together."

Jimmy did a quick dusting, ridding his fingers of food crumbs and extended a hand to his brother nodding cordially again.

Yolanda told Roland, "If you do not shake his hand immediately, I am leaving."

"Where do you think you're going to go?"

"My friend operates a cab, remember?"

"Jesus, Mary, and Joseph. OK, fine. You're my son. But that man you are with, never. He will never set foot in my house."

"Shake his hand."

"I can't." He stretched out his hand however, palm down on the table, and Andrew put his hand on top of his father's and turned to his mother. "Good enough, ma. Good enough for now."

"Amen," she said. Another toast, "To my son, Andrew, who is also Jimmy's brother, and my husband Roland's son."

"To Andrew!"

"And to Allie," said Andrew.

"A good friend is hard to find." Yolanda winked in Allie's direction. "Let's mark this moment with some flan and espresso. Waiter, please."

Lulu and Me

The winter I ran away, I moved into a garret in Province-town, where I wrote poetry under the light of a candle far into the wee hours. Out my window, two stories up, I could see snow glistening on slanted rooftops that led like an uneven staircase to the bay. Below me, a twisted narrow path led to Commercial Street, peaceful and stark as an unwritten page. It was 1973 and I had run to the end of the world as I knew it to find freedom.

I knew Provincetown from spending summers with my dad and Grandma Tess in her cottage in Truro. It seemed she'd lived most of her life since Grandpa's passing as a beachcomber. I liked following behind her when we collected beach glass and she walked barefoot, her skirt hem rippling. From time to time she cast her eyes squinting over the bay while holding onto her wide-brimmed straw hat.

I also liked hanging with kids whose families like mine

vacationed in August in nearby Corn Hill. At least once during our vacation a group of us—Jack, his twin, Pete, Marie and her brother Tim, and I—walked some 20 miles, partway along the beach, inevitably hitchhiking, to see the sights in crazy P-town.

We bought ice cream cones and sat on the Town Hall benches with other tourists to watch the gays sashay by in their tie-dyed tees and tight jeans, blue and red bandanas dangling like flags from their rear pockets as they raised their limp wrists jangling bracelets in the air while calling, Mary this and Mary that. It was a grand circus and I riveted on the vision of guys applying lipstick and eye shadow like feral kisses on one another. The message was loud and clear. In Provincetown, you could be anyone you wanted and do just about anything.

I had envisioned a lifetime of summers on the Cape with Grandma and dad, but my grandmother died suddenly when I was 15 and a year after that, my father took off. When I finally got the wise idea that I could escape back to the place I loved on my own, I also had the crazy notion I might find my father there, hanging among the queens, happy to have found a colorful nest akin to his lost childhood. I knew when we left my mother and brother for two summers in a row that he was prepping for some kind of separation, never dreaming he would just go and never return.

I ran away the November after my 17th birthday, tired of dealing with a mother who was stoned on valium 24/7 and a brother, who at 15 was an acid-head and thief, stealing even from me. I just didn't want anymore of that. When my father was home he'd spread a kind of lightness like sparkles whenever he spent time listening to his jazz albums. He'd go around whistling and joshing like a happy man then, which made me happy too. Without him there, home was a place I couldn't take. I felt too young to be hooked on sadness.

You could only think of a garret stepping into my pyramid-shaped woodsy dwelling in P-town, which was really a stripped attic. It had nothing but a mattress in it and shelves made from found boards and cement blocks on which I set my few clothes, favorite books and a journal. Two windows, tall and beveled, faced east and west, so my room was always filled with either sunlight or moonlight. At $80-bucks a month, I knew it was a rip-off, but it meant the world to me having a place of my own. It's true, what Virginia Woolf wrote, a woman needs a room of her own. That miniscule view of the bay I had from one window was my hook to everything.

I was 17 and traveling light, with only my body and imagination. I thought of my favorite writers then, lying sprawled on my belly while composing poems and journaling in my composition book under the light of a tall, yellow candle. I thought of Hemingway and Fitzgerald, and of Zelda and Hadley and how they made due when their husbands disappeared into drink and literature, and of Anaïs Nin and Henry Miller disappearing into literature and each other. How many women impoverished, full of ideas, restricted by circumstances, had like me written late into the night into the silence of their notebooks, messaging the future.

I didn't know jazz then, save for the record my dad had

bequeathed me at 15, Dave Brubeck's *Time Out*, which I loved, not so much for the music, which was unlike any I had heard to date, but because my dad loved jazz and because I loved him, I therefore loved it. I understand now, years after that time of gestation in Provincetown, that coming to love jazz has always been the journey to my father's heart. In his absence I got into the music, slowly, through the years, finding in it the voice I had missed so much that Bird, Dizzy, Trane, Miles and others all articulated for him so beautifully, the blues of solitary men, alone inside.

The second floor of the house on Standish was Jane's and had a kitchen, bathroom and living room I used, as well as two bedrooms. Jane lived there with her kid Dylan, who was three at the time. She had left a heroin-addicted boyfriend in New York City, and an apartment so tiny, Dylan's bed was the bathtub. Jane always said the rickety house on Standish was heaven next to that, even when the heat didn't work and we walked around like soldiers, shoulders blanketed, taking turns stuffing our stockinged feet deep into the oven's belly, even when taking the uneven, loosely attached wood steps to the second and third floors made you feel you were climbing a tree house.

In the basement apartment lived a cook and his lover, Chris, a fisherman and drunk I sometimes saw slipping out early mornings, leaving a zigzag of prints along the alleyway leading to Commercial Street, which led to the harbor, where he had his tugboat. He always looked the same— black galoshes, yellow rubber coveralls, long-sleeved white shirt, short black hair akimbo. He and his partner always picked the wee hours to duke it out with pots and pans and cries of "you sonofabitch," that surely woke up most in the neighborhood. Although I heard their distant dissonant trouble, I never saw their faces, ever.

Jane and I shared almost everything—joints and meals, conjuring bulgur madness on the stove, grain mixed with peanut butter and honey, stuff so coarse you could barely get it down. We just fixed on the fact it was healthy, so we tossed it into a hot pan and stirred. Dylan climbed the counters, looking for peanut butter and honey which he plumbed with his bare hands. We laughed at our culinary ineptitude and Dylan's ability to stomach just about anything.

Dylan was always running around half naked, as Jane couldn't be bothered changing him. Nights, whenever I was home, he crawled the stairs to my attic space with whatever book he could find so I could read to him. I couldn't read him anything out of Nietzsche, although I did read him poems by Adrienne Rich, and made up tales about heroic little boys and a family living in a cabin in the woods in the snow. Once I read him *Winnie-the-Pooh*. Stories were all I could give him, and I let him curl up next to me. "What," or "read it again," were his refrains. A grimy-faced Cupid, one hand wrapped around his blond curls, another anchored on my stomach, he gazed beyond at the dark window as I read as if it was my very face.

Provincetown in winter was like nothing I'd imagined. Gone the color and mayhem. The only place open for work was the fish factory. I'd never worked with my hands before and the idea of it sent a thrill through me. The only other job I'd ever held was at a gift shop as a sales girl, saving up money to leave home.

Misfits and Portuguese townies who held a proud, long-time legacy to the sea worked with me at the fish factory at the end of Commercial. The old timers with gnarly hands and droopy eyes huddled close to one another in the locker room, eyeing you suspiciously, sure you were up to no good. Nothing you said or did could convince them you were anything but bad seed come to ripen in their town. Of course they knew, having seen too many kids come in from the outside and unravel in their backyard due to drink and drugs. Now there was disco, which was its own kind of drug. By the mid 80s, another decade, half the town would be taken by AIDS, but for now the prevailing belief was we were all ageless and immortal, and there was something like greatness in the wildness we were each determined to sow.

Joe, the geezer who ruled over everybody at the triple F, short for fuckin' fish factory, took one look at my smooth, untainted hands and haughty mane wound up into a bun, and decided straight away to put me through the mill, sending me first to snip the head, tails and backs of scrod on the first floor, then to pack lobster tails on the second, and finally to pan fish for freezing up in the dark frigid recesses of the third floor, all in a day's routine. Nobody ran up and down those rickety fish factory's steps more than me. The townies were right, I saw the job as temporary, chalking it up mostly to experience with a capital E.

It was some kind of nightmare staring mornings into a bin of scattered guts and headless fish when you were hung over, which everybody always was. I caught the blood-shot stares of my co-workers, gay and straight, some barely older, all of whom seemed vaguely familiar from the bar scene the night before, and tried not to pass out from the smell of ammonia that was splashed on the cement floor 24/7 to disinfect and cut the fish odor.

Everyone I talked to had either split from home or was running from the law or both and headed toward some vision of bliss. For some, P-town was just a pit stop. Ellie wanted to save money to live in a commune in Vermont. Jacques, to run a farm. Jorge, to open his own beauty parlor. Stoner and Marnie, to buy a fishing boat and live off the sea on their own. They came from Florida, where they'd grown their own pot and made homemade wine, which they shared with us at break time. My friends taught me anarchy is the only road, authorities exist only to betray, and it's a wild world, baby. I absorbed my new set of commandments like holy wine and hosts.

Trudging home in my pin-striped coveralls and scale-splattered galoshes after work, I stopped at the corner liquor store to buy three shots of bourbon in tiny bottles and a half gallon of Tavola Red, cheap wine. Nobody ever proofed me then, maybe because it wasn't summer, so they knew cops wouldn't check. I took the bourbon down after chewing on a handful of spinach leaves and picking on a can of tuna in my room. Then Ellie came over and we shared the wine, discussing Erica Jong and her book, *Fear of Flying*, which was the rage then.

"You afraid of flying?"

"No. But the book means freedom, flying is freedom. The question is, are you afraid of freedom."

"No."

We are not afraid of anything. Freedom is everything. And we are it, we agree. It's the only thing worth dying for. We are young, we can do anything. It's what I tell myself spinning to "Love's Theme" at Piggies Dance Bar, sure I've found heaven, and that my life will unravel only on pink clouds from now on.

A group of women, hippies, straight and gay, find their way to the middle of the room, form a circle, dance together. I'm the only preppie, dressed in suede boots, jeans and a lambs wool vest over a white blouse. My hair is long and I let it sail, sure of nothing but the night itself into which I let go. My eyes snag flared skirts and bare feet kicking air, flying beaded necklaces, casting higher into deeper darkness behind high beams that crisscross overhead hiding secrets. There I am flying.

I go home with a jazz singer named Lulu, who informs me right away she is bi, a new term. She is living in a trailer on someone's property. Around three am, past all sense of reality itself, after listening to Lulu talk with so much love about music I don't know but my father knew, I step out naked, skipping patches of snow to peek at Commercial Street, to announce I am here, its newborn. The hand-hewn sign to The Hermit, a cellar restaurant just away, creaks spookily in the wind—welcoming or admonishing me? Overhead the sky brims with stars just for me. I crawl back to Lulu, who places both her hands around my own as I curl up next to her under a quilt. "You're crazy, love," she says. I'm not sure whether she means crazy love or crazy, love. Either way, from that moment on the two words, crazy and love, become synonymous.

Crazy is naked late night struts outdoors, stripping and running into the bay after hours, sleeping with whomever you want, laughing at yourself and at the world. Crazy love is Provincetown in winter, where everyone will love anyone just for warmth, a fire and experience.

Sundays we hang in the Back Room before a fire, listening to opera and drinking Courvoisier. My friend Mel who is 40 and came here from New York loves opera and tries to explain it. Even then I know certain music cannot be explained. After the opera comes classical music, then jazz to which I dance, to and fro, thinking of Lulu, creating myself in the moment through movement, dancing to conquer what I don't know. I don't know jazz or how I will move to it, but I am moved by its unpredictability, challenged by it, and unafraid.

Love of music I got from my dad. It was his hand took me to dance classes when I was a kid. I learned about Isadora Duncan from my teacher Miss Jeanine, and about Martha Graham, although it was Isadora I fell in love with, her dancing being like poetry, my other love. As a kid, I danced solo onstage, early on making music my own.

Skipping and turning across the Back Room floor, I am light itself erasing the past making way for the future, unafraid of taking up space, enjoying the feeling of eyes on me. Pockets of men stand together sipping exotic drinks, appreciating my interpretation and expression, and applaud when the song is done. Is it because I have somehow managed to articulate something undecipherable, made sense of something un-danceable, brought the mute out of the closet?

Jazz is as unpredictable as I am, as my father was. And it heralds Lulu, who is even more unpredictable than me, wearing a flower print dress, a beaded necklace and a peasant blouse covered with a fox fur. She raises paint-chipped, nail-bitten fingernails to scratch the air. Lulu who can sing but not dance but is ashamed of nothing and stands before me clapping upward then down, her eyes slightly closed, familiar with the song that bears her name, although I don't know it then. She knows and loves where it goes and what I am doing with it that I don't know. She joins me picking up imaginary broken pieces from the wide-board floor, tossing them up to heaven where they will be made whole, then begins to blow an imaginary horn, happy as I am happy. We are both fixing for a party.

Later, Lulu tells me the song that bears her name, "Lulu's Back in Town," and I begin to connect jazz to flesh, to names like Thelonious Monk, and to the moment that sails into heaven and an emptiness that is full and rich. There is a musician named Monk who like Isadora makes holiness out of the incomprehensible, piecing it all together.

We take off somewhere and later return to the Back Room when the disco ball is swirling and the beat is now. The boys take off their tops as they start to sweat, not caring it's winter, recreating summer heat, which is sexual and endless. The strobe lights deceive us all, hypnotizing those like me who are prey to the most obvious magic, finishing off what drugs and alcohol started. Nobody is sober or straight. Everybody gets too high. The fireplace cackles away, but no one sees or hears it. Only a couple struck immovable, too stoned to move, stretch before it on the floor as if paying homage to a god. Somebody strange, catatonic, eyes frozen too wide, leans like an admonitory ghost against the glass sliding door exit.

Jacob, who we met tonight while dancing, pulls me by the hand, and I pull Lulu and we struggle to slide open the door and slip outdoors, ripping off our clothes as we streak naked into the dark blue silvery frigid bay, our baptism into night which we take screaming. Hurrah. What have we beaten? We have beaten the night, death. We are young, young, and will last forever. Even this ice cold baptism will not stop us. We are holy. Lulu! Lulu! We step out, shake off like dogs and struggle to put on sandy clothes, impossible, stumbling and losing our balance knocking against one another. The bar lights flicker so we know it's last call and have only minutes to get warm before the night's fire goes out for good. As we run back indoors I see two men, no four, smoking in the alleyway, caressing one another, up and down. Now they are one. It's always time for love-making when the bars close in P-town. We are only one body when night finally draws to a close.

"Come with me to New Orleans," Lulu says while we are recovering from hangovers in the Holiday Inn sauna into which we sneak the next day. "For Mardi Gras," she explains. "I can't stand this cold shit much longer. I miss the blues. I miss Mardi Gras." I've heard of Mardi Gras but have not yet heard the blues. We are arching stiffly, reluctantly into January, more winter.

"Months fly by," she says poetically, breaking into a Janis Joplin laugh, full of mischief. Her gut sags a little like she's had kids, but I don't ask, don't want to know. She looks at my flat, tan belly and long legs, eyes burning with what could be desire or envy. Her hazel green eyes are always burning, summery. Although she's only older by five years, her body has been through a century. Pale and soft, she is womanly to me, while I still feel like a girl.

We meet up with Jake at Bradford Gardens for breakfast. Eggs, toast, sausages, and Bloody Marys, the only thing that really takes hangovers away, swears Lulu. The sky is bright blue and we are all wearing sunglasses. I'm skipping work today. It's only hours before the next party anyhow. Jake is handsome all in black, dark, with curly hair. I wonder where he's from and admire a loop in one ear, which he removes and offers to me. "No, no thanks, man." Men are quick to give you anything when you are young. I don't want anything but freedom. Jake wants to go to Canada. It's no longer to escape the draft, so I wonder what he's escaping, but don't ask. There is so much I wonder about, but questions freeze in me. I want to find answers on my own. Besides, music can explain anything. It alone knows everything.

Everyone you meet in Provincetown is a guide, a kind of muse. You spill who you are, what little you know, telling everything right away because who knows what will happen next. Moments fly. We burn so fast, all is lost overnight. And we disappear soon, even if we always wake up to love.

Mardi Gras is like every night in Provincetown thrown into 24 hours. My head is splitting and there's nowhere to escape the party outdoors, even in a room with five people, only one that I know—Lulu. On I-85, near Birmingham, Lulu's 60's station wagon broke down. We left it with a mechanic and hitched the rest of the way with a vanload of partyers. Three days it took, stoned all the way.

In New Orleans, the call of trumpets and drinking never cease. Is this jazz? Is this? It's the one question I now ask and have to know.

"It's all jazz," says Lulu, stretching silkily on the bed, and she means it. I have never seen her looking so happy or so remote, her paleness one with the sheets. In New Orleans, a part of her melds with the very air. She takes her clothes off repeatedly, gyrating once on a balcony, wearing only colorful gold and silver beads and sunlight. I never take off my clothes in New Orleans whose wildness feels foreign and frightens me and is neither young nor innocent. In New Orleans, we are too drunk to do anything but bump into people and spill drinks and listen to music.

In the Allways Lounge on Saint Claude, or some place like it, someone dressed like a monkey makes love with someone dressed as a nun on roller skates right in the middle of everyone and everything. It's two men, theatre like Provincetown. Another time we follow a crowd to Sweet Lorraine's where everyone knows Lulu, Lulu who has never seemed more at home. This is where she belongs. Everybody kisses and hugs and somebody passes her a mike, rightly lifting her like a star onto the stage, where she sings, "'Blue Moon', dedicated to Chase," while gazing at me. I am Chase, I realize, remembering my name. What else do I know?

First piano, then horns, and back to Lulu swinging. Somebody tosses her broken flowers, one of which she arranges in her hair over an ear, so she looks like Lady herself, a white Lady anyway. Drunk and beautiful, in her own space, she reconstructs the song, "You saw me dancing alone …without a girl of my own," looking at me all the while. People bop and sway. The horns come in again. Lulu's voice trails and the crowd pops like a champagne bottle bursting open love.

Strangely, it's then I realize music doesn't always have to make you crazy, like disco does. This music finds its way to a deeper, grounded place, where there is a placid sea of knowing. It's my antidote to the future, although I don't know it yet.

Lulu loses her voice in New Orleans. All the way home, strung out and sung out, we summon images of the sea that we love, hearing it lap against our ears and breasts, remaking us. I dream of how it was even before jazz, my father raising me up to the sun then onto his back when we rode waves home on the sea side on the Cape, me holding onto the chain of holy medals around his neck because his shoulders were slippery with tanning oil, trusting the precarious ride on his back facilitated by St. Christopher and the Blessed Virgin. For seconds, I felt safe, at home, like no one could touch us, until we struck the ground of shore and my father returned to surf the sea on his own. Even then, watching his golden head disappear inside waves, I was never sure he would return, in some way, a part of me always knowing he was destined to go.

Back from New Orleans, we crash for a whole week, sleeping off the damage of alcohol, keeping the best moments of our roller coaster ride. Before we know it, April comes, hammering away, trying to disguise winter's wounds and pretty up Provincetown for summer. It's then, as the town fills with strangers that Lulu slips away, no goodbyes, believing in nothing but going on, going back to the one constant she knows, jazz, which waits for her, and is just now calling me.

Arya F. Jenkins is a Colombian American whose poetry, fiction and creative nonfiction have appeared in numerous journals and zines. Her fiction was nominated for a Pushcart Prize in 2017 and 2018. Her poetry was nominated for the Pushcart in 2015. Her work has appeared in at least five anthologies. Her poetry chapbooks are: *Jewel Fire* (AllBook Books, 2011) and *Silence Has A Name* (Finishing Line Press, 2016).

About Fomite

A fomite is a medium capable of transmitting infectious organisms from one individual to another.

"The activity of art is based on the capacity of people to be infected by the feelings of others."
—Tolstoy, *What Is Art?*

Writing a review on Amazon, Good Reads, Shelfari, Library Thing or other social media sites for readers will help the progress of independent publishing. To submit a review, go to the book page on any of the sites and follow the links for reviews. Books from independent presses rely on reader-to-reader communications.

For more information or to order any of our books, visit http://www.fomitepress.com/FOMITE/Our_Books.html

More Titles from Fomite...

Novels

David Adams Cleveland—*Time's Betrayal*
Jaimee Wriston Colbert—*Vanishing Acts*
Roger Coleman—*Skywreck Afternoons*
Marc Estrin—*Hyde*
Marc Estrin—*Kafka's Roach*
Marc Estrin—*Speckled Vanities*
Zdravka Evtimova—*In the Town of Joy and Peace*
Zdravka Evtimova—*Sinfonia Bulgarica*
Daniel Forbes—*Derail This Train Wreck*
Greg Guma—*Dons of Time*
Richard Hawley—*The Three Lives of Jonathan Force*
Lamar Herrin—*Father Figure*
Michael Horner—*Damage Control*
Ron Jacobs—*All the Sinners Saints*
Ron Jacobs—*Short Order Frame Up*
Ron Jacobs—*The Co-conspirator's Tale*
Scott Archer Jones—*And Throw the Skins Away*
Scott Archer Jones—*A Rising Tide of People Swept Away*
Julie Justicz—*A Boy Called Home*
Maggie Kast—*A Free Unsullied Land*
Darrell Kastin—*Shadowboxing with Bukowski*
Coleen Kearon—*Feminist on Fire*
Coleen Kearon—*#triggerwarning*
Jan Englis Leary—*Thicker Than Blood*
Diane Lefer—*Confessions of a Carnivore*
Rob Lenihan—*Born Speaking Lies*
Colin Mitchell—*Roadman*
Ilan Mochari—*Zinsky the Obscure*
Peter Nash—*Parsimony*
Peter Nash—*The Perfection of Things*
Gregory Papadoyiannis—*The Baby Jazz*

Paolo Valesio/Todd Portnowitz—*La Mezzanotte di Spoleto/ Midnight in Spoleto*
Sharon Webster—*Everyone Lives Here*
Tony Whedon—*The Tres Riches Heures*
Tony Whedon—*The Falkland Quartet*
Claire Zoghb—*Dispatches from Everest*

Stories

Jay Boyer—*Flight*
Michael Cocchiarale—*Still Time*
Michael Cocchiarale—*Here Is Ware*
Neil Connelly—*In the Wake of Our Vows*
Catherine Zobal Dent—*Unfinished Stories of Girls*
Zdravka Evtimova—*Carts and Other Stories*
John Michael Flynn—*Off to the Next Wherever*
Derek Furr—*Semitones*
Derek Furr—*Suite for Three Voices*
Elizabeth Genovise—*Where There Are Two or More*
Andrei Guriuanu—*Body of Work*
Zeke Jarvis—*In A Family Way*
Arya Jenkins—*Blue Songs in an Open Key*
Jan Englis Leary—*Skating on the Vertical*
Marjorie Maddox—*What She Was Saying*
William Marquess—*Boom-shacka-lacka*
Gary Miller—*Museum of the Americas*
Jennifer Anne Moses—*Visiting Hours*
Martin Ott—*Interrogations*
Jack Pulaski—*Love's Labours*
Charles Rafferty—*Saturday Night at Magellan's*
Ron Savage—*What We Do For Love*
Fred Skolnik—*Americans and Other Stories*

Made in the USA
Middletown, DE
17 April 2019